1 | The Mouse Triptych Ian Thomson

2 | The Mouse Triptych Ian Thomson

THE MOUSE TRIPTYCH

Ian Thomson

Claire

Lots of love,

6.vi.13

Cover picture by Catherine Servonat-Blanc

trip·tych/'triptik/

Noun:

A picture or relief carving on three panels, typically hinged together vertically and used as an altarpiece.

A set of three associated artistic, literary, or musical works intended to be appreciated together.

for Lyam

who ordered me to write

A good writer possesses not only his own spirit but also the spirit of his friends.

Friedrich Nietzsche

Contents

A Stroke of Genius

Polemikos

The Downing Street Cat

These stories are entirely fictitious and the mice in them are not intended to represent any mouse living or dead. This is equally true of the human characters.

Copyright © 2013 by Ian Thomson

All rights reserved.

A Stroke of Genius

8 | The Mouse Triptych Ian Thomson

I

This will do admirably, thought the Mouse as he emerged from the corner where the green carpet didn't quite reach the skirting board. Outside it was several degrees below freezing. He had been awoken by the unendurable cold and had slid into the big old house through a broken vent in the damp course. Further along, crumbling mortar had given him access through a gap in the bricks to the underside of a floor joist along which he had scrabbled until, at last, he had come to the draughty runs behind the wainscoting where, judging by the smell and by the droppings, generation upon generation of his forefathers had raced and rootled and tumbled over each other since the house had been built. He had explored these runs tirelessly for several hours, going backwards and forwards over the same ground, passing and re-passing under or behind a number of large holes most of which admitted only a chill and watery daylight into the tunnels through which an icy wind blew. Soon even these ashen patches of light began to diminish and dim until they were as dark as the mouse runs themselves.

But there was one hole which did *not* diminish or dim. It was the largest of the holes, and through it poured light that was constantly changing, now warm and golden, now glimmering and multi-coloured, now flashing black and white. Through it too there poured noise. A most prodigious and terrifying noise. It was mostly a blaring and a booming and a banging, with whistling and screaming, and what might be music, but such music, thought the Mouse, as could only accompany the ending of the world. It left him cowering and timorous, just beyond the reach of the flickering light. And yet, through the hole there also poured warmth, a rich, cosy, fuggy, enveloping kind of warmth which finally sucked him from the maze of corridors where the arctic winds blew and into the room and onto the green carpet.

This will do admirably, thought the Mouse.

For he realised immediately that the racket had not been the prelude to the Crack of Doom but that it emanated from a largish flat screen television which was also, he now saw, the source of much of the flickering light. He made an experimental run along the skirting board behind the television, through tangled wires and ragged dust-clogged cobwebs, and over the husks of long-dead moths and bluebottles, and then back again to just outside the hole.

Now, you might reasonably be wondering how the Mouse came to understand that the noise and the light came from a television. Ah, that - he would have told you if he could - that was for him to know and you to find out.

For the Mouse, you must understand, was no ordinary mouse. He was a chess Grand Master, for one thing, and had even invented a variant on the game in which the queens, in addition to their imperious horizontal and diagonal sweep, could also leap over other pieces in an L figure, rather like a knight. There was some fine-tuning to be done here since the games played with this amendment, though dramatic and bloody, tended to be rather short. He was excessively fond of the music of Monteverdi and Telemann. Furthermore, he was a philosopher, being deeply read in the more arcane passages, back- alleys and cul-de-sacs of the works of Spinoza. His favourite philosopher, however, was Michel de Montaigne and he especially admired the essays *On Vain Cunning Devices*, *On Smells*, and *On the Custom of Wearing*

Clothing. You might ask at this point how a mouse could possibly attain to this erudition, but that says more about your poverty of imagination than the brilliance of his.

The Mouse's name, since you ask, was Maximilian Emmanuel Lichtenheld. And he was inordinately proud of it.

Plucking up courage now, the Mouse made another foray, setting off from the corner and still keeping to the skirting board, he skittered behind a bookcase, over dried flower petals, fluff balls and a foraging woodlouse and then behind an armchair beyond which, to his delight, he found half a poppy seed cracker on the carpet. Standing on his hind legs and balancing on his tail, he nibbled at the cracker, razoring along its edge from side to side. This was good. This was very good indeed. Whilst eating he began to orientate himself. Now, the eyesight of the common house mouse, or *Mus musculus*, is not good, but Maximilian Emmanuel was an *Apodemus sylvaticus*, or field mouse to you, and his eyes were enormous.

And this is what he saw. He saw a prairie of green carpet in whose deep pile were crumbs and hairs. He saw the edge of a thick red rug. To his right alongside the rug, he saw the carved legs of a Dutch oak coffee table, and in the distance he saw a vast armchair, with regency stripes in cream, green and rose. Beside it, he saw a nest of oak tables on top of which was a jug of purple glass which contained huge lilies already shedding their dark orange pollen and emitting their heady smell which he found faintly nauseous, for his olfactory sense was, of course, also exquisite and acute. He sneezed a minute sneeze and preened his gorgeous whiskers with his tiny pink hands. To his left he saw the television screen, with its lurid, shifting shapes of which he could make very little. Beside it, he saw a fireplace, in which he saw a halogen heater, swinging its glowing pink triple bars, now towards him, now away. He saw that the fireplace was framed with tinsel in shimmering red and gold, and in the tinsel were pinpoints of white light which chased each other around the fireplace in ever-changing patterns sometimes slow and stately, sometimes like fireflies dancing. It was, you see, Christmas Eve.

And in the armchair, he saw the Man. Or to be more precise, for Maximilian Emmanuel was nothing if not precise, he saw the soles of the feet of the Man. And they were not pretty. The heels were dry and cracked and the insteps scaly, and there was an angry bunion on the right big toe. The pads were calloused and shiny. His toenails were ragged and horny and one was mahogany-coloured, ingrown and infected. There were grimy cracks between the toes, which made Maximilian Emmanuel wince, for he was a fastidious mouse. Much more of the Man he could not see, but the ankles seemed swollen and dropsical, and there was a glimpse of calves of a lardy white colour and texture, where a few coarse black hairs sprouted pointlessly. He could see the ragged hem of a goose-turd green towelling robe from which loose threads hung.

He watched the Man for a long time, resisting the temptation to jump onto the bookcase for a better view since he deemed it a little early in their relationship to risk exposing himself to notice unnecessarily. He was so very still that the Mouse thought he must be asleep, or maybe even drunk, for he now noticed what he had missed before, namely that there was a near empty bottle of Glenmorangie malt whisky on the carpet by the armchair and that the Man's right hand was resting by his thigh on the seat of the armchair, and loosely holding a cut glass tumbler. He was surprised to see that the hand, though rather gnarled at the knuckles, was clean and even elegant, with neatly trimmed and polished nails, in contrast to those awful feet.

He was musing on this strange disparity between hands and feet when suddenly the Man, with a seismic grunt, lurched upright and the tumbler rolled over the rug, sparkling in the many-coloured light. Maximilian Emmanuel somersaulted in panic and edged backwards but swiftly behind *his* armchair to the space between it and the bookcase from which vantage point, his little mouse heart palpitating wildly, and his sharp little nose twitching, he watched the unspeakable feet move around the room. The glass was retrieved and placed on the nest of tables. The feet crossed to somewhere near the television and first the charming fairy lights winked out and then the noisome roar of the television, together with the bilious configurations on its screen, snapped off. A gratifying silence rushed into the room. The bars of the heater went out and, finally, the feet moved out of the Mouse's range of vision, the table lamps dimmed, a door opened and closed softly, and Maximilian Emmanuel Lichtenheld was alone in the dark, and, since he was a nocturnal creature, this suited him very well indeed.

Yes, thought the Mouse once more, this will do admirably.

No sign of any predators in here, he thought, no scent or sign of dog or cat, not much likelihood of a fox or a mousing owl indoors, and the feet have gone. Time, he thought, for more ambitious exploration.

And so along the skirting board he scurried. His huge eyes gave him fine night vision, his formidable whiskers twitched splendidly and his keen sense of smell urged him towards – food. Soon he came to the foot of a door jamb and since the bottom of the large white door was considerably shy of the surface of the carpet he squeezed under it with ease into the kitchen. That it *was* the kitchen was abundantly clear and it was also clear that the Man, for all his refined fingernails, was a messy cook. The rather greasy linoleum was scattered with food debris: papery brown onion skin, a twist of dried linguine, peas, a few shreds of carrot peel, a scattering of cooked rice grains. Nibbling at the edge of the carrot peeling, the Mouse sat up on his hind legs with his tail stretched out behind him and surveyed the terrain. Opposite him was a range of sturdy looking cupboards, with a fitted double oven whose glass doors were smeared and streaked. A fridge hummed to itself in the corner. The cupboard units did not reach the floor but rested on metal supports a few inches clear of it. Here the linoleum ended and beyond, under the cupboard, was a dark domain no human eyes had seen for years. The Mouse crossed its borders.

This dark domain was overlain with deep, sticky dust. In the middle of it, like a skeleton in a desert, was a rack from a roasting tin which had been pushed under there long ago and forgotten, for it too was mantled with the same sticky dust. The whole eerie plain was dimly lit by the red light from a four socket extension lead shoved under there, more recently he supposed, since it was almost dust-free. Round things had rolled under there, a marble, a mouldering cherry, the ghost of a grape. Unaccountably, near the back wall there was a white bishop from an expensive looking chess set. Maximilian Emmanuel imagined that the Man must have found its disappearance deeply vexing.

The cupboards did not quite meet the wall behind them. He could see a hole in the back panelling which had probably once been gnawed by his distant uncouth cousins, a brood of house mice. He steadied himself on his powerful back legs and with one leap he was in through the hole. On inspection, the Mouse could see what kind of furniture this was. It had begun life as a flat pack. Handsome and solid looking on the outside, its interior was no such thing. The chipboard shelves were held up with plastic studs which fitted approximately into roughly bored holes in the side panels. One stud had fallen out and had been replaced with a bit of broken pencil so that the shelf above it was at a shipwrecked angle. His reconnoitre of the interior of the cupboards was swift and expert. He squeezed through gaps in the flimsy structures, jumped over pots and pans, skittered over crockery, and at last wriggled through a tiny aperture up into – a stock cupboard.

Oh, brave new world!

Cinnamon, cardamom and cloves, in sticks, pods and nails; lovely whole nutmegs; peppercorns black, green and pink; sunflower and sesame seeds; flour and sugar and salt – but all of them in Kilner jars of various sizes or Tupperware boxes. He hurdled over jars of parsley, sage, rosemary and thyme; slalomed round soy sauce, light and dark, Worcestershire sauce, red wine vinegar, white wine vinegar, sherry vinegar, balsamic vinegar until he came across a jar of clover honey. He licked a thick dribble on the outside for a while, then noticed a little hessian sack marked 'Herbes de Provence'. The hot fragrance filled the cupboard but it was the sack itself that promised a toothsome snack, until – out of the corner of his eye – he saw it: a field mouse's heart's desire, his El Dorado, his Shangri-La, his Happy Valley, his Utopia: a crumpled but virgin packet of Old Fashioned Quaker Porridge Oats, once purchased no doubt as part of an intended regime of healthy eating, but nudged to the back of the cupboard by more interesting comestibles. How did he know they were Quaker Oats? Goodness, what juvenile questions you ask! Do you imagine a Mouse that has read the Essais de Michel de Montaigne *in the original French* would have any difficulty reading a cereal packet?

In no time at all his incisors had razored away a corner of the packet releasing a chalky avalanche of its crunchy treasure. Maximilian Emmanuel feasted, yes, in solitude, but like the Holy Roman Emperor of Mousedom.

Some considerable time later, when he could eat no more, he thought that it was time to find the wherewithal to make a nest and to get some sleep. It is true that in less exciting times what is the middle of the night to you would be the middle of the day to the Mouse, but he had been through mighty exertions over the last few hours and the food had made him drowsy. He dropped through the hole at the back of the cupboard and then squeezed himself with some difficulty (for his furry belly was very full) between the back panel and an ill-fitting side panel which twanged so sharply behind him that he thought at first that it had caught his tail. This compartment was quite different from the treasure house above. It smelt of oil and paraffin and turpentine. There was a bag of nails, light bulbs, one marigold glove with a squashed tube of superglue stuck to one finger, a hammer, Duraglit, beeswax furniture polish, binliners, a black knight from the same chess set, some grimy rags and any number of dusters, used and unused. None of this was in any order but had simply been stuffed in there any old how. However, in the midst of this jumble, there were two, blue, spanking new, kitchen scourers in their original polythene packaging. You know the kind – a wiry mesh pad backed with coloured foam. The very thing, thought the Mouse gleefully. He made short work of the polythene and then deftly shredded the foam backing from one of the scourers shaping it swiftly into a luxurious nest. He sat in the middle of it and then, curling himself into a ball with his tail wrapped around him, he fell into a deep and dreamless sleep.

The battery of the kitchen clock which had been losing time for weeks finally gave out and its sumptuous tick was stilled. A deep, thick, fuzzy silence filled the Big House from the roof-tree to the cellars. For it was Christmas Eve, you see, and nothing was stirring. Not even a mouse.

II

Maximilian Emmanuel slept until Boxing Night. He had woken at some point and thought he could dimly hear the trumpets and kettledrums of Bach's Christmas Oratorio and the chatter of many human voices coming from next door, but he couldn't be sure and was soon folded again in black and furry sleep. In the end, it was hunger that woke him, and he stretched full length in his blue nest, turned around a few times and clambered up to the store cupboard where he enjoyed a substantial breakfast of Quaker porridge oats though he stopped short of the rather ill-bred gourmandizing of two nights ago. Fully refreshed, he zigzagged down through the cupboards, dropped into the red twilight of the Plain of Dust where he could see his footprints from Christmas Eve quite distinctly, and out onto the linoleum of the kitchen floor. To his surprise it had been swept and mopped though he quickly found a raspberry that had rolled into the middle of the floor and had been camouflaged by the pattern in the lino. He nibbled and sucked at this for a while, sitting up on his haunches watchfully, until he noticed that a quantity of milk had been spilled by the fridge. Abandoning the rest of the raspberry, he sipped at this gratefully for he was very thirsty.

The kitchen was dark but for the faint red glow and no artificial light came from under the door either. He slunk under it. It was very quiet in the study. The curtains were open and lozenges of anaemic moonlight fell on the carpet from the two high windows. The feet must be out.

Now curiosity may have killed the cat (and good riddance to the noxious beast, thought the Mouse) but Maximilian Emmanuel was no less inquisitive, if rather more circumspect. Here was the perfect opportunity for a thorough reconnaissance of this drawing room, or study, for such he took it to be. He passed into uncharted territory, though still keeping to the skirting board, and passed behind another book case, under a radiator, over another thickly woven rug, in front of a large desk with a chair pulled up to it, sharp left and under one of the windows, where he found a fluff-coated peanut which delayed him only slightly, until he came at last bang up against yet another bookcase.

He leapt decisively onto the middle shelf for a browse. After all, 'a man is known by the books he reads'. He registered in order: *Item*: *The Satires, Epistles and Ars Poetica* in Latin by Quintus Horatius Flaccus, Loeb Classics Edition, rather battered. *Item*: Shakespeare's *Sonnets*, Folio Society, excellent condition. *Item*: A handsome Edwardian Tennyson (Oxford). The old paper smelt scrumptious and the Mouse jumped on top of it. He observed that even after a century some of the pages were still uncut and he was tempted to lend a hand, or rather his teeth, towards trimming them but in the end he decided to deny himself this seductive little snack in favour of further research.

Leaping back onto the shelf he perused the spines of: *Item*: Thomson's *Seasons*, half-bound in pigskin, eighteenth-century by the look of it, a gourmet edition, thought the Mouse, for whom the expression 'to devour a book' had been invented. Then some battered paperbacks: *Was There Another Troy? New Irish Poems* by Billy Clarke; *Ecce Homo*, Nietzsche; *The Symposium*, Plato, and two pristine hardbacks in their crisp dustcovers: *Practical Tortoise Raising, Philosophical Essays* by Simon Blackburn, Oxford University Press, and *Republic Unvisited* by L.R. Todd, Cambridge University Press. By the Lord Harry, the Mouse concluded, the Man is both literate and a philosopher, despite his abominable feet.

From the bookshelf, Maximilian Emmanuel could see that a voluminous sofa occupied the centre of the room and that it had the same regency stripes in green, cream and rose as the Man's armchair. The desk he had passed earlier was positioned behind it so that anyone seated at it would be facing into the room whose walls, he could now appreciate, were a deep tasteful red. It was a prodigious leap from the shelf to the cushions along the back of the sofa but to a rodent of the Mouse's dexterity it was a mere trifle, a bagatelle. All the same, he ran backwards and forwards a few times along the thick braid which edged the cushions, with his tail erect, as if doing a kind of lap of honour. He nibbled at the braids a little, loosening the threads, sat back on his haunches, stroked his whiskers and leapt onto the desk.

Unlike the kitchen floor, the desk was scrupulously clean, polished even, and immaculately tidy. At one corner was a desk lamp of classical design with a cream lampshade trimmed with gold, and at the other a standard lamp which also had a cream shade. There was a pine book rest supporting an open exercise book covered in crabbed and crippled handwriting but, even standing on tip toe with his front paws on the ledge of the book rest, he couldn't read it, so execrable was the script. There was a rather beautiful art deco decanter, with indentations in the shape of shells around the base and the key pattern around the top, containing, as the Mouse guessed, fino sherry as pale and bright as healthy urine. Beside it was a sherry glass with a few drops at the bottom in which, despite the time of the year, there floated two tiny flies. There was a Panasonic cordless phone and a metallic red Dell laptop whose screensaver was a photograph of the self-same laptop which contained a photograph of the self-same laptop and so on in a pantomime of infinite regression. Beside it was a large, plain black mouse pad with a cheap-looking Microsoft mouse on it. As if to teach it a lesson for impertinence, Maximilian Emmanuel kicked it around a little with his hind legs as a horse might kick a fence. A red light came on inside it.

Everything on the desk was absolutely foursquare and shipshape, including the broadband router which stood next to the phone. It was aligned precisely with the back of the desk and the back of the sofa. What was odd was that a printed card had been clumsily sellotaped to the front of the hub below the four green lights and that the card was at a slight angle. The Mouse pattered over to read it.

Across the top it read: Police Link Officers for the Deaf (PLOD). Below it were printed what must be the Man's name, address, mobile number and email address, and below this were a number of statements each with a square box next to it. They read: *I am deaf; I am hard of hearing; I am deafblind; I am deafened; I am speech impaired; I work with sensory issues; I use sign language; I lip-read; I use written notes; not applicable.* The Man, or someone else, had ticked the box which said: *I am hard of hearing* and also a box against a statement which read: *I agree to the police keeping my details for emergency contact, the 888999 service and the National Emergency Text service.* Then he had signed it with an impenetrable hieroglyphic. Across the bottom, in large bold text, white on blue, it said: Emergency Text Access - For deaf people and speech impaired people. Police – Fire – Ambulance – Coastguard – Rescue. Your password is: 0SFLN5. Then in blue on a white panel: 888999.

So that was it. That explained the infernal volume of the television. Quite a satisfactory evening's sleuthing all in all. He was sharing a house with a partially deaf man of letters who was chronically untidy in the kitchen, but suffered from Obsessive Compulsive Disorder when it came to the surface of his desk. He was a philosopher and an alcoholic, who was fond of raspberries. And he had deplorable feet.

Maximilian Emmanuel leapt from the desk to the chair to the carpet and, keeping to the skirting board, for he was not overly fond of open spaces, he made his way back to the kitchen, to the cupboards and back to the delectable mound of spilled porridge oats.

III

He did not see the Man again for several days. On holiday perhaps? In the bosom of his family? With a maiden aunt in Eastbourne? With a mistress in Paris or a camera and a catamite in Tunis? Maybe he was in hospital having those atrocious feet seen to. In any case, he had the house to himself without fear of a sudden encounter with the Man. He made only one attempt to expand his territorial range, sniffing and whiskering around icy bedrooms, a dank and draughty hall where thick green textured wallpaper was curling upwards from the skirting boards and there was the sour odour of damp. There was a chilly utility room with soap powder on the floor and sacks of onions and potatoes leaning against a chest freezer which he thought he might return to when this interminable winter was over. He missed the warm fug the Man had provided but passing along the bottom of a door leading to the garden he could smell the cold outside and was grateful to return to the comfortable regime of the study, the kitchen, the cupboards and the porridge oats. Most of the time he slept and dreamt of hedgerows and hayfields.

And then, around what you possibly, and I certainly, would call Twelfth Night (the Mouse's favourite play, incidentally), this peaceable state of affairs came to an end. There was no sudden epiphany, of course. Just the sudden roar and shriek of the television bursting into life and, over a couple of hours, an appreciable, and appreciated, rise in the temperature of the house. A brief sally into the study confirmed the return of the feet.

Now this did not bring very much in the way of change in the Mouse's lifestyle. If anything the comfortable warmth led to even longer periods of tranquil, furred slumber; the supply of porridge seemed inexhaustible, and the Man's untidy cookery often supplied interesting titbits to vary his diet, a shred of apple peel, a sliver of cabbage, a splash of cooked lentils, and once, a whole fish finger at which he nibbled and gnawed until it was discovered and removed two days later. Encounters with the Man himself were infrequent and uneventful; the Man was usually an early-to-bed-early to-rise phenomenon while the Mouse was a creature of the night. On the rare occasions where their paths did cross he doubted very much whether he had even been seen. If he suddenly saw those feet on the green carpet, it was a matter of reflex to whisk himself down the nearest hole and vanish utterly. In any case, given the Man's fallible hearing, so the Mouse surmised, his vision was probably rather hazy.

And so the Man and the Mouse lived together but quite independently in the same house. Weeks passed and outside the snows melted and turned to black ice, glacial winds rattled the skeletons of the trees, and the pipes froze up.

But Maximilian Emmanuel had been wrong. He *had* been seen and he was to find this out very dramatically one evening. He was nibbling away along the edge of an old copy of The Times (Saturday, October 30, 2010: AL-QUAEDA 'BOMB RUN' PUTS WEST ON ALERT) which had been slipped behind the somewhat stained stainless steel pedal bin when suddenly there was a deafening clang! Obviously his scrabbling at the newspaper, which was serving at once as tuck and possible bedding, had been a trifle overenthusiastic and he had been heard. The Man had hit the metal bin with a metal instrument, perhaps a ladle, with considerable force. To Maximilian Emmanuel, with his delicate and finely tuned hearing it was as the clangour of doom. He nearly ran up the wall. He turned to disappear down the hole in the corner where the bin was placed and, behold! - it was plugged with wire wool. The Man clearly knew of his cohabitant. Very well. Who was it who said a mouse does not rely on just one hole? Plautus, was it? However, the nearest alternative was under the cupboards, and this would mean that the Mouse would have to strike a diagonal across the linoleum on the kitchen floor, and he hated that. But there was no other option. He streaked across the lino at prodigious speed as the man hurled the ladle at him.

All this had taken but a few seconds. As the Mouse lay on the Plain of Dust, his tiny heart thrumming wildly against his ribs, he could see in the grime that he had skidded the last few centimetres, and he could see too, gleaming out on the linoleum, that it had indeed been a ladle that had been flung at him. As his heartbeat slowed to its normal rapid rate, the Mouse reflected on what had happened and quickly concluded this: the Man was afraid of him. He had sneaked up on the pedal bin and, rather than whip it away, and hope perhaps to catch him by surprise and perhaps splatter him with the ladle, he had, rather squeamishly warned him by striking the bin. Nevertheless, the Mouse knew he would now have to be exceedingly circumspect. His escape was not going to be the end of it.

Nor was it. The very next evening, after breakfast, Maximilian Emmanuel Lichtenheld emerged for his daily survey of his territories. The hole behind the pedal bin had been unplugged and beside it stood a mousetrap – the spring-loaded kind with a bar which was intended to snap over and break his spine or crush his skull as he took the bait, or to shatter his ribs and leave him paralysed and in agony for several hours until his eyes dimmed and he blessedly expired. He smiled wryly, or would have done had he been a Disney mouse. The trap was baited with a piece of cheese which didn't tempt him in the least – a piece of anaemic waxy Cheddar of the very cheapest kind. Did the Man really think he was going to risk his life for *that*? A morsel of creamy Reblochon, maybe. A salty smear of St-Augur, perhaps. Or maybe a nutty little cube of Manchego might have seduced him into an act of daredevilry and bravado. A little dollop of peanut butter might have done the trick, or a smidgeon of mincemeat, but Cheddar? *Cheddar?* He sniffed haughtily and resumed his tour of inspection.

His strategic review revealed what he had suspected. Outside four critical boltholes, including the one in the corner by the television, there stood one of these miniature guillotines, each one baited with a scrap of rubbery cheddar. It was laughable, of course, but all the same the Mouse recognised it for what it was – a declaration of War, nothing less. It was absurd that a hulking human should be so afraid of a tiny mouse that he would go to the trouble of installing such an armoury of death machines. Well, he could ignore them, of course, and picture the look of bemused disappointment on the Man's face as he checked them daily and found them persistently rodent-free while the cheese gradually became green and mottled. But no, this called for a statement of intent, an act of defiance and scorn. He returned to the trap behind the pedal bin, stationed himself behind it on the 'safe' side where the man would have held it between finger and thumb to set it, faced away and kicked out with both powerful hind legs at the edge of the wood. It sprang immediately with a mighty snap, lifting slightly from the linoleum and twisting. He turned to inspect it in triumph. The offending cheese had leapt from the pin on which it had been spiked. Rather than eat the stuff, the Mouse carried it to the hole and dropped it down. He wanted the Man to find the trap in the morning, sprung, corpseless, and baitless.

At intervals during the night, he sprang the other three traps and disposed of the cheese. The next evening, the traps had been re-baited and re-sprung. This time, he triggered them on consecutive evenings, disposing of the cheese on each occasion. He relished the Man's inevitable puzzlement, and these tomfooleries were fair enough, you know, because after all, the man was trying to kill him.

This continued for perhaps a fortnight or so. The traps were set and sprung and a great deal of Cheddar vanished. There followed a sort of truce. The traps did not reappear and the Mouse wondered if the Man had given in and had decided to tolerate their coexistence. He rather thought not, for he had sensed the Man's fear, smelt it almost, and did not think he would rest easy unless the Mouse were annihilated. And he was right. A few days after the cessation of the Battle of the Mousetraps, the next phase of the Man's campaign was revealed: Operation Venom.

During a nocturnal recoinnoitre, he came upon a small plastic tray, dark green and rectangular in shape, about seven centimetres by nine. In it was a pile of dark grains which smelt exceptionally toothsome. However, Maximilian Emmanuel also smelt a rat (though I doubt if he would have put it like that). It really was just too, too wretched. Why would the man want to feed him after attempting to snap him in half with those barbaric traps? It made no sense whatsoever; therefore it was pitifully obvious that this was an attempt to poison him. In effect, mind you, there was no call for even such elementary reasoning, for the Mouse had noted earlier a conspicuous red and yellow packet, propped by the pedal bin, which bore a picture of a lightning flash striking the image of a mouse. It was labelled RODENTICIDE EXTRA and bore the legend: EXTERMINATE!

He had examined the instructions in fine print which read:

'Place up to 20g of Rodenticide in the bait trays provided. Position in protected locations where mice are running and feeding, e.g. under cupboards and behind furniture. Inspect bait at appropriate intervals, i.e. every three to seven days and replenish until no more bait is taken. Search for and remove rodent bodies at appropriate intervals during treatment. All waste should be double-bagged using bin-liners or

> *similar before disposal in a bin with a secure lid to prevent accidental poisoning of dogs, cats and birds, foxes and other wildlife.'*

'Treatment! Waste!' The Mouse was outraged. 'Bin-liners!' And how scandalous that the lives of dogs, cats, birds, foxes and other vermin should be esteemed more highly than that of Maximilian Emmanuel Lichtenheld! Heresy!

The Mouse checked his supply lines, his lines of communication and retreat, and sure enough, next to two other spots where the shifting of the old house had opened up holes in corners between the skirting board and the floor, there were two other bait trays each with its charge of savoury death. How to respond? This was not easy for his counter-offensive must not be counter-productive. He had considered just kicking the trays over but two things weighed against this: one, the debris would be scattered in his habitual itineraries (and you already know that the Mouse was a most fastidious mouse); and two, he might accidentally become contaminated with the poison and fall ill, and he could not afford to fall sick in the midst of battle. He must needs have his wits about him.

Gradually, a strategy framed itself and settled in his mind. He would do nothing for several days; nothing at all for, perhaps, a week. He imagined the Man checking everywhere for his desiccated corpse, but there would be none. He would return, again and again, with increasing frequency and growing despondency, to find the bait untouched, and he would be vexed and frustrated. The thought caused the Mouse's whiskers to positively whirr with delight. (I have used a tinge of poetic licence there for, of course, his schadenfreude was quite noiseless).

Over the next few days he maintained his plan of non-engagement, but it began to prove fearfully difficult, contrary to his expectations. In one respect, it did have the desired consequence, for he saw from time to time that the trays had been moved, rather pointlessly, a few centimetres here and there, as if to fine tune their lethal allure. But the delectable aroma of the bait, the tantalizing bouquet, the savoury tang in the air was everywhere. It was a siren smell. It drew him, his nose twitching convulsively, it drew him to the brink of disaster. Just a grain or two, his nose told him, just a little amuse-bouche would make no difference. The poison would be too dilute to have any discernible effect. No, no, no, said his brain. That is precisely what the enemy wants. Resist at all costs.

You know enough about Maximilian Emmanuel Lichtenheld by now to know that in the end, after sore torment, his brain over-ruled his nose. This was not the moment for shilly-shallying. It was time now for decisive action. He decided. He acted. He defecated conspicuously beside each of the three trays, leaving his droppings as a declaration of defiance and contempt.

By the very next evening the bait trays had gone, but so had the porridge and this is how it happened. The Mouse had awoken to a fearful banging and clattering and scraping in the cupboards above his nest and thought it prudent to make himself scarce. He dropped down the back of the kitchen fittings, and there, beyond the Plain of Dust were the feet, but not just one pair. The Man's repugnant hooves were there sure enough, but they were some way back from the foot of the cupboards. Closer to the units was another pair, surely belonging to whoever was wreaking such havoc up above. They wore battered mauve slippers trimmed with bedraggled synthetic fur and white ankle socks over deep tan surgical stockings. A woman then. A neighbour? Probably. He needed a better vantage point and he needed to get away from the cupboards. Assuming the enemy were wholly engaged in whatever it was they were doing, he slunk across the dust and out into the open, keeping tightly to the wall and at right angles to the cupboards until he came to the gap between the fridge and the wall. This would afford him a retreat should he be spotted.

He needn't have worried. The Man and the Woman were totally absorbed. Sitting on his haunches just by the refrigerator, he could see that she was removing everything from the top shelf, packets and jars and Tupperware boxes which she then handed to the Man who placed them on the work surface behind him. She appeared to be having some difficulty reaching to the back. The Man's feet disappeared and reappeared a few moments later. A metallic squeal and a click and the four rubber feet of a little aluminium stepladder were placed alongside which the slippers mounted as far as the third step. More jars and bottles and packets were handed over, the herbs and spices, the sauces, the oils, the honey, all of it. These the Man either wiped clean or dropped with an apocalyptic clang into the pedal bin.

This was scorched earth stuff. They were cleaning out his storehouse, stripping his granary.

Eventually, with an oath, the Woman handed down the packet of Old Fashioned Quaker Porridge Oats with the sizeable and jagged hole that the Mouse had gnawed out of one corner and the chalky oats streamed from it as she and the Man tried to catch them. The rest of the oats, perhaps a third of a packet, would have fallen through the hole as she had picked it up and remained as a dune at the back of the cupboard. With more angry clattering, the Man rooted about in a lower cupboard, and produced a grimy plastic dustpan and brush with cobwebs and hairs matted in its bristles. He handed this to the Woman, whom the Mouse now noted was wearing a white print cotton frock covered with enormous purple peonies. She began to sweep out the floor of his larder with puritanical vigour, and the banging and clattering in the corners created a cloud of oat dust which set the Man sneezing.

By now the Mouse had had quite enough and was keen to make an exit. This was no problem and there was barely any need for his customary caution. If he had marched past the Humans on his hind legs playing a tuba they would not have noticed him, so absorbed were they in trying to eradicate every last vestige of his presence.

Nonetheless, the Mouse sloped judiciously by and on into the study and it was now that he discovered that the bait trays had been removed, along with his own ironic tribute of droppings. He discovered something else too. Every mouse hole that the Man had been able to find had not only been plugged with steel wool but the unforgiving stuff had been plastered in position with domestic cellulose filler. The filler was no problem in itself – he could eat through that in no time, and quite tasty too, but the steel wool was an effective barrier, or would have been. The fact of the matter was that the number of holes accessible to the Man amounted to less than half of those available to the Mouse. The underground still functioned, though some stations were closed. However, the study was warm and cosy and so he decided to lie low while the Humans were busy. After snacking on the edge of a copy of Philosophy Now magazine which was lying by the sofa, he carried shreds of it behind a bookcase, where he made a temporary nest, curled himself comfortably, and drifted into a nap where a perfumed breeze wafted gently across a shimmering meadow of silver and green.

IV

He awoke some hours later to darkness and silence. Or silence overlaid with the ticking of the radiator as it cooled for the night. The Mouse returned to the kitchen cupboards to see what, if anything, could be salvaged from the raid. The Plain of Dust was as he had left it, illuminated by the soft ruby light and crisscrossed now many times over with his neat little footprints. Dust had settled over the slide he had made when the Man had thrown the ladle at him and the white bishop lay on his side in dusty indignity.

He jumped up into the back of the cupboard and scrambled into his storehouse. It had been scrubbed clean of the rings from jam jars and the crusted spillages from flour and paprika - and porridge. The porridge had gone, of course, along with much else. Nothing had been put back that had not been wiped spotless and, indeed, much of the provender in there was new with the maddening plastic intact around the tops of jars and bottles and with packets still wrapped in cellophane. Even the walls had been scrubbed and scoured and there was the powerful smell of some lemon detergent which brought on a fit of sneezing. There was room to move around now and the Mouse did a quick inventory of the stock. Nothing palatable or accessible, alas. The porridge had not been replaced for obvious reasons. There was a bag of dried prunes and a packet of chocolate biscuits which were not without appeal but they were right at the front of the cupboard and the Mouse was not keen to be surprised at table by the sudden opening of the door.

He dropped down to what had been his nesting box to find that it too had been gutted and swabbed, tools neatly packed in a wooden box, nails and screws in clean jars, bottles of turpentine and disinfectant wiped or washed, and nothing, nothing at all nestworthy. Not that this cupboard offered a secure refuge anymore; it was too tidy and too open. The Woman had done a good job.

Maximilian Emmanuel had to admit to a sneaking admiration of these manoeuvres. They had been drastic and they had been thorough. However, the Mouse was not in the least downcast. He would take up residence behind the bookcase, a more fitting dwelling perhaps for a philosopher. There would be no worries either about nutrition. He was sure he could rely on the Man's slovenly kitchen craft to guarantee a floor strewn with delicacies whenever he prepared a meal. He remembered the utility room too and scampered into the hall and along a narrow corridor, always hugging the skirting board, and under the door where a washing machine was groaning and throbbing and shuddering. Sure enough, by the freezer were onions in a red string bag, a thick paper sack of potatoes, and when he jumped onto this to investigate, he was able to see, on top of the freezer – oh rapture! – a box of apples. Maximilian Emmanuel was not going to starve in this best of all possible worlds.

So, there followed the Cold War – a kind of hostile truce where each was aware of the other, yet neither made much of a move. The feet were in evidence sometimes as routines overlapped, though not the slippers. The Mouse, for his part, deliberately left a spoor which said: catch me if you can, but I'm still here. This would comprise nibbling on the edge of a letter on the doormat, a few discreet droppings on the bathroom scales, or gnawing at the wiring. This latter offensive resulted one evening in a lamp going out by the armchair in which the Man had been reading. It could simply have been a bulb expiring, of course, but in any event it elicited a roar of outrage from the Man which the Mouse found greatly diverting.

Gradually, it became less cold in the hours when the central heating was off. The halogen heater was removed and stored, the Mouse had noted, under the stairs. Each day was a little longer and sometimes there was even sunshine. It shone through the dusty windows casting lozenges of light on the walls, which travelled around the room as the day lengthened. And as the days passed, they glowed lower on the red walls until eventually there were rhomboids of light on the green carpet too. The Mouse found himself more and more alert and needed to sleep less. He expanded his territorial range to include an austere dining room, where a candle end on the mantelpiece afforded a tasty snack, and a built-in hall closet which was a good place to nap. Things had become rather routine and uneventful.

Until, that is, he came face to face with the Man. And by this you must understand that I mean, quite literally, face to face – not face to feet. For the Mouse had emerged from under the kitchen door one fine evening to find that he was looking right into the Man's face. He froze in his tracks, as well he might, for the face (compared with his) was enormous and terrible. You see, the man was lying on his side on the carpet, stricken. The Mouse ran for cover behind the television but the man did not move. He waited. He waited for quite a long time, but nothing happened. The Mouse thought then that he might perhaps be dead. With infinitesimal care, he crept forward again.

Something grotesque had happened. The Man's face appeared lopsided, or rather, it appeared as if his face had collapsed on the left side. His lip and eye looked as if it had been pulled down on that side and the skin of his forehead there seemed very smooth compared with the natural wrinkles age had brought to the other side. A trail of slobber ran from his mouth and mucus from his nose. His left eye too was watery and ran. At the moment, both eyes were open, and it was starkly evident that he could see the Mouse, but could not move to do anything about it. There was a look of abject terror in the eyes, so helpless and so very intense that the Mouse was shocked and disgusted.

Then the Man tried to get rid of the Mouse in the only way he could – by closing his eyes. The right eye closed completely but the left eyelid barely moved. Instead, the eyeball seemed to roll upwards and disappear behind the affected eyelid.

The Man lay there paralysed. The Mouse saw now that he had suffered a stroke. How did the Mouse know this, you ask? You should have realised by now, dear reader, that there are more things in heaven and earth than are dreamt of in *your* philosophy. And besides, Maximilian Emmanuel was clearly conversant with Black's Medical Dictionary.

The Man lay there paralysed, making anguished, wordless, glottal cries. He was entirely in the Mouse's power and they both knew it.

Now, strange to relate, the Mouse had a sudden urge to dance. He moved closer to the face. This was after all the creature who had tried, with ruthless determination, to kill him. This was the creature who had tried to cut him in half, to poison him, to starve him. This creature (the Mouse did a rapid calculation) was five thousand times his weight and now he was lying helpless before him. And this creature could see the Mouse perfectly well. The Mouse wanted to dance a dance of triumph and insolence before his very eyes, to punish him for his unmerited malice. He wanted him to sup full with horrors.

But the Mouse did *not* dance. The Mouse began to think. He gazed into the rheumy eye and saw the fear there and he thought that though the fear was irrational it was very intense fear. And he thought that the fear was what had driven the Man to try to murder him, not any ingrained malice. Nor could the Man have known that he, Maximilian Emmanuel, was no ordinary mouse, but the very paragon of mousehood. And then he thought that to dance in front of this paralysed creature in order to terrify him further would be beneath his dignity. It would be to descend to the Man's own feral reflexes.

Much better to leave him there and get out of his sight lines, he thought. Much better still, would be to *help* him. And why should he help his would-be assassin? Because he could. Because of a superfluity of being, the privilege of a free spirit – because he could.

But how could he? This was rather daunting. Clearly he could not physically move the Man, and, despite his extensive medical knowledge (for he was a renaissance mouse), he could not administer any palliative care, not least because any contact with him would result in the Man's going into spasms of dread. Whilst he was pondering the magnitude of the task before him, he heard a buzzing from somewhere beyond the sofa. It was an intermittent but insistent noise, like a bee with asthma. Yes, I know that bees buzz with their wings, but the thought is charming and neither the Mouse nor I wish to dismiss it. (You are an exasperatingly literal-minded reader, you know.)

The buzz was now accompanied by chimes in descending thirds. The Mouse leapt onto the Man's shoulder, from there onto the sofa, up onto the cushions, and thence onto the desk where he could see a Blackberry whose vibrations were causing it to swivel between two knots in the polished wood of the surface. The viewing panel read:

'1 missed call 13.49 Sat 01 April 01522772488'.

It stopped as suddenly as it had begun and the Mouse became aware that the Man was crying out in inarticulate fear. Leaping onto his shoulder must have scared him out of his wits. Simultaneously, the Mouse became aware of the blue and white card taped to the internet hub directly in front of him, which read PLOD: Police Link Officers for the Deaf.

Now the Mouse *did* dance. He danced on the Blackberry's keypad. He danced out 888999. And when the phone chimed back with the text message: 'Enter your password now', he danced out 0SFLN5. When it politely asked: 'Which service do you require?' He danced out A-M-B-U-L-A-N-C-E. And he danced out the Man's name and address when the phone requested him to. Finally, he read: 'An ambulance will be with you shortly. Please stay by your phone.' The Mouse stepped onto the black mouse pad and did an extended little dance of self-congratulation. You may find this hard to believe but that is how it was.

The Man was quiet now. He could have no idea of the tremendous thing the Mouse had just done for him and that was the way it should be. Maximilian Emmanuel jumped from the desk to the arm of the sofa and from there onto the windowsill to await events.

It may have been a quarter of an hour later, maybe twenty minutes – the Mouse would later claim that it seemed more than a decade – when he heard sirens and then three men in black puffer jackets with green and white day-glow bands across their chests came up the drive. They rang the doorbell, and again, and again. They couldn't get in! The Mouse bounded from the windowsill, to the desk, to the sofa, to the bookshelves, and again, round and round in sheer panic and frustration. Find the slippers, he thought, find the Woman. She's a neighbour. She's bound to have a key. He shot back onto the windowsill full of a plan he couldn't communicate. However, it proved wholly unnecessary for at last one of them came over and tapped the window and the Mouse leapt like greased lightning onto the curtains.

Maximilian Emmanuel could see the paramedic peering into the room, one hand over his eyes to reduce reflection. He called over a colleague and the Mouse realised he had seen the Man. Now, there were two young faces looking in as he swung on the curtain out of their line of vision.

Things began to move very quickly. There was a sequence of very heavy thuds, then the sound of splintering, and then a crash as the front door (presumably) fell into the hallway. The Mouse dropped to the carpet and skittered around the room to his reality checkpoint behind the television, keeping to the skirting board all the way. Within moments three pairs of black rubber-soled shoes, and trousers with a vertical green and white strip walked into the room. They knelt and examined the Man. Then they lifted him with infinite gentleness onto a stretcher, covered him with a white blanket and fastened leather straps around his thorax, abdomen and thighs. In a matter of minutes they and their burden were gone.

The Mouse imagined how puzzled they must be as to how a man in his condition could possibly have raised the alarm. The hero of the hour would have grinned from ear to ear if he could, but instead he preened his beautiful whiskers.

V

The man was gone for about three weeks and was returned in a wheelchair. The left side of his face still drooped so that his mouth looked like a permanent scowl. The slippers appeared daily to attend to his needs and to feed and clean him. Evidently, he had been rescued but not much restored.

He was always there now, and he was not aesthetically pleasing, to say the least, with his gurglings and his dribblings, and quite often he would soil himself and the stench would be noisome. He had never been what you might call good company, what with the murder attempts and everything, and now the Mouse thought it was high time to go. Youth must be served, he thought.

And one day, in late April, he did. He disappeared into the unblocked mouse hole at the corner of the Plain of Dust, and ran along the ancestral tunnels, scrambled upside down under the floor joist, and emerged through the crumbling mortar in the gap between the bricks into the garden. The air was sweet and balmy. Late evening sunlight slanted in glowing bars across the grass. Pear blossom drifted, white and light. The Mouse felt an obscure stirring within him and he knew what it meant. It was time to make a real nest out of dried grasses rather than synthetics, smelling of earth not turpentine. It was time to find and woo a female. It was time to sire a brood of mouslings. The long light shook across the lawn, pigeons moaned, and the blackbird trilled his thrilling song, as Maximilian Emmanuel, in the violet hour, skittered over pebbles and snails under the hedgerow, in search of love.

Polemikos

Some months later, Otto Rupert Emmanuel Lichtenheld was having his Latin Lesson.

'This is well boring,' he said.

'Why is it boring?' asked his father, Maximilian Emmanuel Lichtenheld.

'It just is. It's so slow.'

'Aeneidos II is not slow. That is not the consensus of the ages.'

'That's just the point. It's not relevant. What has Virgil got to say to a mouse of my age?'

'I should think he has just about everything to say to a mouse of your age. The tale of the Trojan horse is always relevant. And it should be particularly relevant to you, Otto. Since one of your ancestors was there.'

'For real? Where?'

'Why, at Troy, of course. His is also a tale that has been passed down the ages. By word of mouse, as it were.' He chortled to himself. 'Do you wish to hear it?'

'Yeah, epic, man.'

'Epic indeed.' Maximilian Emmanuel smiled thinly. 'Very well. This is how the Trojan mouse, Polemikos, told his own story to his nephew, Sminthos. Attend.'

I

No-one remembers his own birth does he? It's strange that your own story has to be begun by someone else. My mother was very beautiful but I suppose every boy thinks that. She it was who told me how she had been hoisted into the hollow belly of the horse in a basket of black bread where she had given birth to me in a nest of shavings tucked into a joint of the curved timbers. She told me never to forget that I was a Trojan mouse and that my father was a hero who had spent a whole night gnawing through the sword belt of Achilles. The next day it snapped just as he was about to spar with Patroklos and the hilt of his sword had dropped on Achilles' big toe which had driven him into a violent hissy fit, noteworthy even though he was famous for his tantrums. Achilles was a cissy, my father had said, and Patroklos was his boy whore. Ah well, he's dead now, burnt on the beach and his ashes were mingled with those of Patroklos and buried on the plain of windy Troy.

But I am running ahead of myself as old mice do. All this business of the horse was a long time ago, a year and a half perhaps. We mice do not live long, but time runs fast for us and our lives are full of action and there is much to remember. This is why I am trying to remember it all for my great-nephew, Sminthos, before it is too late. My back legs are arthritic, the fur on my right haunch is gone where it was burnt away on that terrible night in Troy, I have half a tail, and I am nearly blind. One night soon an owl will have me and I will go into the dark with my father who was caught by Patroklos' hound and thrown by the tail into the campfire by Achilles. Sminthos tries to look after me but it cannot be long. That is why, as he swings on the reeds where the River Scamander chuckles over its pebbles, I am telling him the story of the horse before it is all forgotten. To the east lies the rubble of Troy, its towers topless no more. You are welcome to eavesdrop.

Of course, I could make little sense of it at the time, and it is only over the months that I have pieced together what was happening. I cannot read and I am not ashamed of the fact. Reading is for philosophers and eunuchs, women and Greeks. But I have my memories and what others have told me. Not many escaped the firestorms that consumed Troy that night but we have shared what we know. Here then is the tale of Polemikos, the Trojan Mouse.

II

We are born blind, pink, helpless and hairless. I was the oldest of a litter of six, a sister and four brothers. When, after a few days, I first opened my eyes, home was a nest of wood shavings inside a dark wooden vault or cylinder which was built like the inside of a boat. There were mighty ribs of maple bent skilfully and they were overlain with louvred planks. The cavernous insides smelt sweet and resinous because this wood was of sawn fir, felled, so my mother had learnt, on the banks of Mount Ida. My mother told us that we were in the belly of a gigantic wooden horse which had been built where it would not be visible to Trojan lookouts down amongst the masts and rigging of a thousand ships. My mother and father, expert scavengers amid the tents of the Greek camp, had seen from a distance its legs grow upwards within scaffolding like towers. Later, the hollow torso where I was to be born, with a trapdoor on the underside, was hoisted and fitted expertly onto the legs. The maple spars which slotted through holes in the underbelly reached high into the vaulted interior. Later still, the beautiful carved head and proud arching tail were secured. Innumerable hides were used to coat the body and fixed with brass studs, the head and tail painted in Ionian white and gold. Great clusters of red garnets were used for its bolting eyes and its nostrils were rimmed with silver. I don't think my mother could have seen all this in detail but it must have been the talk of the camp. You may have been told by some Cretan liar or other that the horse was built overnight by Epeus and Athene but that's cobblers. It was three weeks in the building, and the finest shipwrights and engineers were involved. Sure, the blueprint was down to Lord Odysseus and they were certainly helped by Pallas Athene – we mice are more pious than men – but I was born, suckled, weaned and active in there long before it was dragged up the beach and wheeled onto the plain. And I was an adolescent before the Greeks climbed up through the trapdoor and we all went up to windy Troy of the many towers.

My father had been cremated in the campfire, poncy Patroklos skewered by Hector, and Achilles mincing amongst the shades of Hades, before the horse was dreamed up by that crook Odysseus. When the time was ripe to provision it for its last night, jars of wine were winched up through the trapdoor, together with a mess of cold cooked beans and peppers in olive oil, and a vast basket of black bread where my widowed but pregnant mother had been feasting. It was to be another four weeks before forty men climbed the rope ladder into the body of the creature, because the cowardly Greeks had been arguing about who should take the perilous ride inside the hollow horse and bring about the doom of Troy. Each man wanted to grant the other the honour. In the end the yellow sons of whores drew lots. By then the bread was mouldy, the beans fermented, and I was a boy who wanted to be a soldier who would avenge his father's death. My mother had named me Polemikos which means 'warlike'.

On the night before Troy fell, though its towers had survived ten years and a thousand ships, my greatest journey began. It was early evening when our cage of wood was filled with light and the voices of men. I was not a stranger to light, not exactly. Our comfortable darkness was pierced with seven shafts of light from what I later realised were spy-holes. There were two in the shoulders of the beast, looking towards Troy, two in each of the flanks looking out on either side onto the tents, and one wittily bored to form the horse's anus, looking out to sea beneath the horse's tail.

At this point in my tale, little Sminthos shivers with laughter, and the reed he is clinging to bends low. Here I must remind him and you that I had no sense of these perspectives at the time, though I learnt much from the men as they waited inside the great horse.

The deluge of light as the trapdoor fell open was blinding and terrifying, as was the sudden blaze of noise from the camp. We mice ran to our mother and clung to her in panic – yes, Sminthos, me too, despite my military ambitions. Then, before the first man appeared, she did something very strange, something without which, Sminthos, you would not be here. One by one, she carried my siblings in her mouth, to the anus of the horse and dropped them through, starting with my little sister, the runt of the litter.

Now, I had often looked through that hole at night, through the forest of rigging that slapped against the masts and whose bells tinkled as the brine gurgled and foamed with the incoming tide. I had seen beyond the ships the vast brooding expanse of the wine dark sea, and above, the black dome of the sky fretted with millions of sparkling, pitiless stars. And I had looked down from that unimaginable height from the arsehole of the horse onto the dirty white sand below. Was my mother mad? Was it possible that my brothers and sisters could survive that headlong fall? We are light and our bones are supple, but from so high? I could understand that she was stirred by the fear of men, who were even now, climbing the rope ladder with uncouth shouts. A man had killed my father after all, even if it was that sulking pansy, Achilles. It crossed my mind, even in the horror of the moment, that any Greek down there, who was not wholly engrossed in the embarkation of the soldiers, might have seen the great horse shitting mice.

Now only I, Polemikos, was left. I was too big to be carried but I would have done my mother's bidding, perilous as it was, if she had told me to jump. We would have dived together, with a prayer to Apollo Smintheos, the Mouse God, either to our deaths or freedom. But it was not to be. She had just turned from the hole when the head and shoulders of that gangster, Odysseus, appeared. I was on the same beam that ran beneath the hole and less than two metres away. We both froze as Odysseus stood upright and took the arm of the next man on the ladder, who turned out to be the hairy thug, Menelaus. (Oh, I was to learn their filthy names soon enough during the hours we spent together in the bowels of the horse.) Weapons were passed up next, long-handled spears for throwing, and spears for thrusting with iron heads and brass butt spikes. These were stacked upright in pyramids on the floor of the horse's belly, ready for immediate use. Massive, circular shields followed, faced with brass and decorated with images of wild animals, boars and foxes mostly. My mother and I stared at each other paralysed with dread. After all, I had never seen a man before and she had good reason to fear them. Suddenly, illogically, my mother began to run towards me. Instantaneously, Odysseus swivelled. He was holding his dreadful brass sword in his right hand and with lightning speed and with keen precision, he cut my mother in half.

Then, casually, laughing, with the tip of his sword he flicked the two halves of my mother out through the trapdoor onto the protesting heads of the Greeks below.

III

I vomited in shock. But there was no time for mourning her; I was in peril of my own life. Infinitely slowly, so as not to catch Odysseus' eye, I retreated into an angle at the junction of a lateral beam and a curved vertical, where, in a fit of boredom, I had earlier gnawed a sort of recess. If I curled myself up tightly and kept perfectly still I might hope to escape Odysseus' keen eye and instant reflexes. As I lay there still quivering, I began to reason. What to me had been an avalanche of light, was to them Stygian gloom and, better, the evening light was beginning to fade. If I remained motionless till night, I might be able to escape down the rope ladder. A mortal leap from the horse's wooden sphincter held little appeal now. Darkness and Patience must be my friends.

Now, with much arguing and shouting, more Greeks began to emerge into the body of the horse. I cannot describe to you, Sminthos, how appalling these creatures seemed to me, I, who had never seen men before, save at a distance through the spy holes. They were, of course, thousands of times bigger than a mouse, so vast that it was not possible in this space to take in one of them as a whole. They were naked apart from woollen cloaks, though each carried a plumed helmet with varying degrees of finery. Each of them had been covered all over in olive oil and their limbs glistened in what ambient light there was. Along each flank of the horse's ribs a bench had been built into the wall and there each man sat as he arrived, his hands on his knees, legs apart, disgracefully revealing his dark genitalia. Their knuckles were red and raw from boxing. Many of them bore battle scars and a number had fresher wounds, some, I noted, as they clambered through the trapdoor, on their cowardly backs. And they stank. The horse had stood for many days now and the wood had warmed and the air inside was close, but as more and more men came in, what with their meat-breath, oil and sweat, and their filthy stinking feet, it became foul and rank.

Suddenly there came a bellow of rage, and a cacophony of shouting and swearing from just below the trapdoor. A handsome but sour-looking lad was pulled up bodily by the hands of the men nearest the trapdoor who had left their benches to see what was happening. He began shoving and pushing.

'What insane bastard did that?' cried the boy. 'What misbegotten, raving son of a bitch did that?'

'Did what?' asked Menelaus.

'Cut the ladder! Cut the pissing ladder! What deranged freak did that?'

I am sorry, Sminthos, but these men were soldiers, and that is how soldiers talk.

I was soon to learn who the peevish boy was. This was Pyrrhus, son of Achilles, and a more evil wretch never walked the surface of the earth. He was just fifteen, the same age as Achilles when he first set sail for Troy.

In the confusion that followed it appeared that one side of the rope ladder had given way leaving half a dozen men swinging wildly while one had fallen and broken his neck. Pyrrhus had been about to scramble in just as it happened. Menelaus and the others attempted to calm him as Odysseus knelt by the trapdoor and examined the damage. The top of the ladder had been attached to two brass rings set into the wood with intricate knots such as only sailors know. One rope was secure on its ring, the knot sealed with tar. On the other ring was a spray of loose fibres just below the tie.

Odysseus stood and faced the boy. They were about the same height despite the difference in age. He said:

'The rope has not been cut. It has frayed. It snapped.'

'You liar,' screamed the boy. 'You pissing liar. You always lie. Everyone knows you are a lying leprous dog. You lied to my father about this war.'

'Your father couldn't wait to get to Troy,' said Odysseus and grabbed the boy by his long hair thrusting his head back. He may have been short, but he was wiry and very strong. 'Now get this. This is my idea, boy! This is my task force. This is my fucking horse, and you do one thing to jeopardise this enterprise and I will hurl you out of that trap door by your pampered arse. The rope snapped.'

'Take your hands of me, you Ithacan prick,' shrieked Pyrrhus.

Odysseus struck him then, with the back of his hand, with a blow that would have felled a full-grown man, and a big one at that. Pyrrhus was hurled to the floor of the wooden cage. Everyone fell silent. Odysseus may have thought up the strategy of the horse but everyone knew that the oracle had said that if Troy were to fall, Pyrrhus would be necessary to the enterprise.

Pyrrhus wiped blood from his mouth and muttered under his breath: 'You'll pay for that, dwarf. If it takes ten years, you'll pay for that.'

Now, despite my grief and terror and despair, I felt a strange shiver of elation. Not only did it do me good to see these ill-bred Greeks fighting amongst themselves, to see the son of the killer of my father laid low, but I knew what had happened. Odysseus was right. No-one had cut the rope ladder,

In the days before the men came, I had often seen my mother gnawing at the rope beside the thick brass ring. Hemp is not a particularly choice item in our diet, though we will eat most things, but it is excellent for sharpening the teeth. Though there were coils of rope and twine all over the place inside the horse, it had never occurred to me to ask why she would go back to that bit so often and, indeed, I often joined her in gnawing away at it. We mice are busy, inquisitive creatures and few of us are given to reflection. I was just copying her, I suppose, as youngsters will.

Could she have known what she was doing? It seems unlikely, doesn't it? I suppose she might have heard rumours of the dark purposes for which the monstrous horse had been brought into the world, but to delay the embarkation, hurl a man to his death, and set Greek against Greek so effectively – how could she have planned this? Naturally, none of this occurred to me until much later. In any event, the atmosphere inside the horse was taut as a bowstring and I was thinking only of saving my hide.

During the chaos, I had jumped to a less exposed location, on a great crossbeam of oak. From here, I could see but not be seen. There was a great deal of shouting and arguing as a new rope ladder was brought from the ships, pulled up with twine, the old one cut away, and the new one secured to the brass rings by Baios, Odysseus' helmsman, the only seaman amongst them. He had to work quickly because the light was fading fast. Then it had to be tested from below by a throng of men swinging on it and declared safe. Teucer, the archer, and slimy Calchas, the seer, were the last to climb up into the horse.

Now, Odysseus ordered that the mouldy bread, now swarming with weevils, and the scummy fermented beans be thrown down through the trapdoor.

'We will do this fasting,' he said.

No-one spoke. But when he ordered that the wine be poured out onto the sand and fresh water drawn up there were howls of protest.

'Tomorrow night, brothers, you will slake your thirst on Trojan blood.'

This all sounded mighty heroic and the sort of thing you might find in an epic poem, but it was really no such thing. Only Menelaus and Pyrrhus wanted to be there, Menelaus to get back Helen, his slut of a wife, and Pyrrhus because he was mad. Odysseus just wanted to get the whole thing over so he could get back to his family. The rest were pressed men, weaklings and chicken-livered quitters, though there were kings and princes among them. All this I worked out from their arguing and bickering.

At last the rope-ladder was hauled up and the trapdoor pulled to and fastened. By now it was almost dark and though I could see well enough I imagined the men could see little of each other and nothing of me above their heads. Odysseus said they might as well get some sleep. He told them that while they slept, the whole Grecian fleet would strike camp, up sail and leave the bay. The lookouts in the high towers of Troy would hardly believe their eyes when they saw the ships departing, leaving nothing on the beach but the fatal horse. Odysseus doubted if the Trojans would come out of their gates for a while. There had only really been skirmishes since the death of Achilles and they were cautious, but come out they would once the ships had gone. And the Trojans were obsessed with horses.

Then, it would be up to Sinon's craft and guile, Odysseus said. From what he was telling the men, I thought this guy sounded like the only real hero among these gutless wonders. He was going to be left behind as a double agent, let himself be caught by the Trojans and spin them a tale. He would say that the Greeks had had enough of war and gone home and left the horse behind as an offering to Pallas Athene. If they swallowed this, he would say that the horse had been built to such a vast size so that the Trojans would never get it through their gates. He would tell them that there had been a prophecy that if the Trojans were to bring the horse into the forecourt of Athene, the goddess would desert her allegiance to the Greeks and favour

Troy. Asia would over-run Europe under her command. Odysseus said such bait would be irresistible to the vainglorious Trojans.

The fur on my back rose at such a slur on my people.

'Bollocks,' muttered someone in the dark. I could see that it was Meges, a spindly red-head with acne who was sitting on the bench next to Pyrrhus. 'No-one's going to believe that corny stuff. They'll rip Sinon apart as soon as they find him.' I have to say that, at that particular moment, I had to agree with him. It seemed a pretty long shot. There were too many 'ifs'.

'Or sacrifice him to Apollo,' said another.

'Who's to say they won't light a fire under this bleeding horse?' came another voice, gaining courage. 'I know I bloody would.'

'Right, and we'll all be roasted to buggery.'

'Yeah, burnt offerings. Ten years, ten chuffing years, for this!'

The murmurings grew to a cacophony of mutiny and dissent. Meges' words had had the effect of poking a stick into a hornet's nest.

'SHUT THE FUCK UP!'

Pyrrhus was on his feet screaming.

'One more word from any one of you and I'll slit you from your navel to your gizzard. Do you hear me?'

There was immediate silence. They were all terrified of this deranged teenager and his rages. Odysseus pulled him gently down.

'Do not underestimate the naivety of the Trojans. They will want to believe this,' he said calmly.

My hackles rose again. I wished he would stop talking like an oracle.

'And now you will be silent,' he continued. 'Once they see the ships leaving, we have no idea how long it will be before they send out spies. Get some sleep. We have a long wait. Tomorrow night we shall bring down Troy.'

See what, I mean, Sminthos. Thought he was the voice of the gods, he did.

Well, silence did descend then, inside the horse at least. We could hear distant shouts from the ships for some time, then nothing much, though with my keen ears I thought I could just distinguish the crash of the waves on the beach and then their sucking withdrawal, raking the pebbles. Then gradually, the snoring began, a brutish noise. I did not suppose they were all asleep. Indeed, I could see that Odysseus was wide-eyed, keeping watch, leaning on his sword. All the same, I trusted to the snoring, to edge along beams and joists to take a look out of the anus of the horse.

The beach was deserted, the tents all gone. How swiftly they had accomplished this! The wide sea was black, except where waves unfurled and broke in white foam. A huge moon rode high in the sky, occasionally veiled by scudding clouds, then suddenly revealed to light up a bright silver highway across the water. And everywhere, everywhere across that broad expanse the moon illuminated the sails of the tiny ships as they approached the horizon, like a thousand ghostly moths.

IV

Though we mice are busy in the night-time, Sminthos, the last few hours had been harrowing, and I believe I slept on and off through that dreadful night trapped inside the horse. There were certainly dreams, dreams threaded with panic, mice fleeing a burning hayrick, mice being devoured by snakes with bloodshot eyes, whose tongues lapped and flickered in their hissing mouths, streams of mice being trampled by a great horse with smoking nostrils which came stamping out of the sea. And in between these fitful nightmares I awoke to the bovine snoring and fetid stench of the men.

Then, as the dawn light leaked through the seven holes in the barrelled body, there were muffled voices raised in argument outside and below the horse. The wrangling woke the Greeks one by one. I could not distinguish any words but thought they must have caught Sinon as planned and that he was not having an easy time of it persuading the Trojans that the horse was an offering to the goddess. Inside the two rows of men sat facing each other in tense silence, each man staring into the eyes of the man opposite him, straining to hear what the Trojans were saying. Odysseus sat, wound up like a coil, with his forefinger to his lips, his eyes red-rimmed and burning.

Suddenly, there was a great cheer from outside the horse, and then silence. The tension was almost tangible.

Then Meges let loose a loud and rancid fart. He looked around him as if for approval and then began giggling squeakily like a schoolboy. Not for long. In one movement, Pyrrhus hauled him up by his hair, turned him so that he was behind him, and with his right hand pushed his short, broad-bladed sword up deep between his ribs. Meges dropped without a sound, stark dead. Quite casually, looking at no-one, Pyrrhus sat down again and began wiping the blade on the edge of his white woollen cloak. No-one spoke.

The shouting outside resumed and then sounds of digging could be heard faintly, the slice of shovels in the sand together with various thumping noises. Soon, there was the sound of brisk sawing, and then the slapping of ropes against the neck and body of the horse. Eventually, after several hours of this, the whole monster suddenly dipped forwards, then slowly and unevenly began to move. Judging by the light from the spyholes it must have been around noon. It was only much later, Sminthos, that I learnt that Sinon had prevailed and that the Trojans had set sliding rollers under the beast, thrown ropes around its neck, forelegs and body and that a great part of the population of Troy, along with troops of live horses, were drawing the great wooden horse up the beach and across the plain towards the city. I could hear prodigious shouts of 'heave!' as the horse moved, sometimes quite smoothly, but more often in violent lurches. And then too, there were other sounds, eerie and nerve-jangling – Trojan women and boys chanting hymns to the goddess – now high-pitched, now deep and wailing – hymns to appease the wrathful virgin-warrior, grey-eyed favourite of Zeus.

In the smelly entrails of the horse silence prevailed. Most of the men sat with their heads bowed, their elbows on their knees, but Odysseus was alert, head back against the timbers, listening like the fox he was, while Pyrrhus looked straight ahead, his ice-blue eyes gazing into some appalling future where his infected soul would exult in nameless atrocities. As the horse pitched and rolled all that morning like some outlandish vessel, the timbers creaked and groaned, while the heat and humidity grew as the unseen sun climbed.

Already, the body of Meges, was beginning to stink. The blowflies, blue-black and fat, arrived first, settling on his sightless eyes, his mouth and his tongue, massing on the sticky blackening wound in his chest and on the end of his penis. Then came the huge sarcophagus flies with big red eyes and black and white striped thorax, and white squares on their abdomens. They swarmed over the acne on his face and chest, and I could see, though the men could not, that they were laying eggs in his flesh. This seething activity was in contrast to the stillness of the men and eventually seemed to draw Pyrrhus out of his distraction. He watched the flies with evident satisfaction and a faint smile played on his cruel lips. Then he stood up and pissed copiously over Meges' face and torso. The flies rose and then settled again immediately, busying themselves with even greater relish. Pyrrhus sat down again and watched spellbound.

At last, after intolerable hours, the horse jolted to a stop. The men in its innards watched each other intently, eager to speak, to chatter. Was this a good sign or a bad one? Where in fact were they now? But all remained silent, cowed by Odysseus' command and in fear of that psychopath, Pyrrhus. Then, quite suddenly, there was silence outside too. The chanting had stopped, the tambourines were stilled, the flutes and pan-pipes hushed. So quiet was it that, even from inside the horse, we stowaways, mouse and men, could hear the wind keening across the plains.

Quite as abruptly the silence was broken by something quite different, the chink of metal on metal, scraping and tapping, and soon rumbling and ground-shaking thuds, Gesturing to the soldiers to remain silent, Odysseus moved up to the spyhole in the shoulder of the horse. After a few moments, he raised his fist and punched the air in a universal gesture of triumph. A muttering of men's voices outside rose to an industrious buzz, and soon there were shouts of excitement and encouragement, seeming to come from below, beside and even, somehow, above the horse. The chanting resumed now, more frenzied and ecstatic than before and war trumpets began to blare, close by and in relays into the distance, where they were joined by the mystical wailing of rams' horns.

Crouching, Odysseus returned to his bench. The men leaned towards him to hear what he had to say. He spoke in an urgent undertone, though the clamour outside was rising.

'They've fallen for it. They're pulling down the Scaean Gate stone by stone to get the horse through. They will draw it into the city and up to the Temple of Athene. Tomorrow, boys, we will feast in the ruins of Troy. But for now...'

Crouching again, he moved to the rear of the belly of the horse where he drew back a tarpaulin which revealed a wicker basket covered with a cloth and a broad-necked amphora. From the basket he handed round flat ovals of unleavened bread, and from the amphora he ladled out water into wooden bowls which had been stacked at the side. The men complained that the water was brackish and the bread dry but they wolfed it down anyway. Later, I was able to run unnoticed between their legs and nibble on the crumbs and sip at the spillages. It would be a long time before I ate again.

After what was probably no more than a couple of hours, there was a great cheer from outside, and the war trumpets brayed again and again. With a momentous lurch which sent some of the men reeling, the horse began to move again.

We were on our way up to Ilium, the sacred citadel of windy Troy. My city, Sminthos. My city of a few hours.

Now the men were at the spyholes in the shoulders, flanks, and arse of the horse, crowding each other and taking turns to see the city they had besieged for ten hollow years. I ached to see it too but hid in the shadows. I had no desire to meet the fate of my father on the blade of one of these thugs and would wait until my time came to escape the horse and somehow do my part in the defence of the city. I mused as to how I could warn my countrymen of the Greek cancer in their midst.

The horse moved more smoothly now on the broad paved highway that led through Troy town to the complex of palaces and temples in its high-towered citadel. Its progress was attended by ever more eerie and ecstatic chanting and the roar of the crowds was a terrible thing.

Just as suddenly all fell silent and the execrable beast came to a halt. Once again, Odysseus put his knotty finger to his thin lips and the men crept like curs to their benches to wait. After a while, we heard a girl's voice, high and clear, so strange and distant it might have come from the moon. It was joined presently by an unnerving chorus of girls' voices, singing responses, somehow voluptuous yet chaste at the same time. It was a hymn to Athene and as ambiguous as the armed Virgin herself.

Beguiled by this magic, the verminous Greeks nearly betrayed themselves, for as the horse began to move again it tilted at a sharp angle with its head raised. Later it became clear that it had moved onto the steep ramp that led up to the temple of Athene, but the moment the floor of the horse moved into this abrupt incline the pyramids of weapons towards the head collapsed with a great clang and slithered noisily towards the rear, where half a dozen men also slid from their benches into a farcical heap and the stinking body of Meges slithered to join them.

If a mouse could laugh, Sminthos, I would have roared.

Their confused howls of protest were quelled immediately, however. Pyrrhus had moved so fast nobody had seen him. He stood motionless holding a great spear, his right hand high on the hasp, his left ready to guide the point into the flesh of the next man who might alert the Trojans to their presence. The little ambient light from the spyholes highlighted the underside of his raised arm, his right flank and thigh, as if he'd been limbed with gold. A boy should not be beautiful like that, I remember thinking. There was something wrong about it.

The racket went unnoticed, however. It was as if the Trojans were drugged. And who could blame them. The parasitic Greeks gone after ten long years of leaching the life out of the city, so many Trojan princes slaughtered, the plain soaked in the blood of boys and men, trade and commerce stillborn and the very air stifling and introverted. And now this gifthorse would appease the vengeful goddess and turn away her wrath. Or so they thought in their intoxication, and I, poor mouse, was the only Trojan who knew of the impending horror which would soon spill into the holy precincts of the guileless city. I sat amid the beams of that infamous icon, Sminthos, and wept and chewed my own tail for very frustration.

The horse now glided on its rollers to its final halt. Men at the spyholes whispered that we were at last in the sacred forecourt of the temple of Pallas Athene, that a bloody sun was setting in a boiling of dark clouds, and that the people of Troy were preparing a feast.

Odysseus counselled sleep and this was welcome to most.

'Let the silly Trojans eat and drink. Let them be sodden and glutted. Before the dawn so much as touches the peak of Mount Ida, they will learn that this gaudy night is their last. Sleep now while the silent squadrons sail back from Tenedos. Soon we will meet our comrades at the ruined gates.'

Before long, the band of butchers was lost in dreams of carnage, their brutal snoring drowned out by the tumultuous din outside as the Trojans unwittingly toasted their doom. Even Odysseus slept, his head resting improbably on the shoulder of a snorting Menelaus. I wondered if he slept with one eye open as the shark is said to do. I do not think Pyrrhus was asleep. He sat immobile holding a spear upright between his parted legs and his forehead leaning on the shaft, his eyes on the floor of the vault. Perhaps he was praying to insatiable Ares, the warmonger, hated by gods and men, and by mice.

V

Ever so tentatively, I moved to the spyhole at the horse's right shoulder. If Pyrrhus was looking down, I would move overhead. The scene beggared description. The temple forecourt was vast but the temple itself was titanic. Its apex scraped the sky. The eight monumental pillars of the façade were white as were the figures in relief on the pediment and frieze, but the background was the deepest cobalt blue. In the centre of the pediment was the goddess, robed in a darker blue with borders of ochre and black; before her she held the aegis, a great round shield of gold in the centre of which was the head of the Medusa with a black, gaping mouth and blue and gold serpents writhing in her hair. The divine image was attended by warriors with blue and gold shields and red plumes on their golden helmets. On the frieze were fabulous beasts, splendidly painted in the brightest colours, hydras, chimeras, giant scorpions, two headed serpents, and treading them all down was Perseus, naked but for a blue Phrygian cap and sandals, both with gold wings. In one hand was a golden scimitar and in the other, once again, the Medusa's head. The temple was guarded by two gigantic gryphons with blue wings and red crests.

Rows of lamps hung from the frieze and over the face of the temple there played the lights of torches and lanterns and of fires blazing on tripods and in braziers. Incense rose in clouds.

Can you imagine, Sminthos, the impact of all this opulence on one who had known nothing but the filthy midden in which he had been born, the reeking vault which was the belly of the horse? I do not think you can, young mouse. It was a revelation, an epiphany – as if the goddess herself had stood before me, naked as she stood before Paris.

A mouse's nostrils, Sminthos, are fine. In the fraught hours, but two moons and a sun, these men had had to piss and shit and it had amused them to defile the hideous body of Meges by using him as a latrine. The busy flies multiplied. The stench was infernal. I hated these coarse Greeks and wanted to escape into the incense-charged air outside where the jubilation was working itself into frenzy. The music had grown in volume and complexity and swirled and crashed in a whirlwind of trumpets, psalteries, harps, timbrels and stringed instruments – and cymbals, loud cymbals, high sounding cymbals. Now there was dancing too, the spinning, orgiastic dances of Asia which whirled the dancers into a trance. To the incense was added the rich, fatty smell of roasting flesh.

This all lasted many hours as I crouched at the horse's right shoulder until, eventually, the revels faded, the music diminished to the doleful complaint of a single flute, and the throng ebbed away to their homes, or fell into a drunken stupor where they lay, there in the temple forecourt. Four lads, reeling and baying, manhandled a half-naked girl past fires which had sunk to embers through the moon-washed streets. The flute throbbed a little longer and was silent. And in the silence, the unforgiving stars wheeled on.

It must have been the silence that roused the men. Pyrrhus sat upright and listened. Odysseus lifted his head from Menelaus' shoulder with a look of distaste and roused him. Down the lines, shakes and nudges woke the slumbering thugs. Suddenly Odysseus stood up and moved towards the spyhole and I only just had time to swing beneath the beam and, I hoped, out of sight.

I had to give these Greeks credit for one thing: they began to move about the vault deftly, quietly and efficiently, arming themselves and each other, fastening a strap, passing along shields and spears, donning their high-plumed helmets. They now stood waiting as Pyrrhus knelt and drew the brass bolts on the trapdoor which dropped open on its leather hinges with a sharp crack. I waited in the desolate hope that the sound in the night might have alerted the Trojans but only thick silence prevailed. The men, too, waited, tense and primed, refreshed by sleep and sharpened by fasting. The light was dazzling to us though it was only thin, reflected moonlight, ghastly on those callous faces. Pyrrhus beckoned Menelaus forward. It had been agreed earlier that he should be the first to set foot in the city as the most wronged by Paris and Helen. He threw down the rope ladder and disappeared, followed by Odysseus. They would lead a party to the demolished gates to welcome the Grecian armies who would have sailed back from Tenedos in the treacherous night.

One by one, the men disappeared through the trapdoor, until all that remained in the horse was the putrid cadaver of Meges - and a mouse.

Pyrrhus had been the last to leave and I was in no hurry to follow him too closely. His father had killed my father, and though I hated him keenly, I had no wish for Achilles' son to have an opportunity to despatch me. I waited a good ten minutes before I scampered to the edge of the hole in the horse's belly, saw that there was no-one at the foot of the ladder, ran down the rope and dropped, rolling a little, onto the forecourt of the temple of Pallas Athene in Troy. Mighty Virgin! It was paved in polished marble – the whole vast square was paved in polished marble, lustrous in the moonshine, as if it were giving off its own light. Had the wealth of this city been what the Greeks coveted all along, and all the tales of violated guest rights and honour just a pretext?

I sat on my haunches by one of the horse's great carved hooves and took my bearings. To my surprise, all of the men had disappeared, all but one, whose sword, helmet and breastplate caught the light fitfully. It was Pyrrhus. He was moving from group to group of sleeping Trojans and cutting their throats in their sleep, men, women, children, their blood black and copious in the moonlight. A stifled moan or a rattling gasp was all I heard as he stalked amongst them, covering their faces with one hand and slicing through their throats with that thirsty sword, as if he willed himself the sole avenger of his father's death.

Mesmerised, I watched the slaughter, helpless, useless, pathetic. At length, I saw the marble paving begin to glow and flicker red, and I realised I could hear the crackling of flames behind me. I turned and saw the Greeks coming up the long paved ramp and flooding into the square, Menelaus and Odysseus at their head, an army bristling with spears, brandishing swords, bearing torches which flared and smoked. Up the gradient of the wide thoroughfare they came and kept on coming and yet strangely quiet they were. Behind them, I could see that houses and public buildings were aflame. I saw Teucer and others firing blazing arrows onto the sloping roofs of the palaces of the princes of Troy, the many sons of old king Priam. On they came, innumerable.

I now became aware of men shouting and the screams and wailing of women, as the crackling and spitting of flames turned into a roar. Still, the Greeks came streaming on, filling the temple forecourt and filing into the broad avenues and narrow side streets that led from it. Befuddled Trojans woke, staggered to their feet, and were cut down. Trumpets began to sound everywhere, proclaiming to the heavens the bloodlust of the Greeks, and the alarms of Troy betrayed.

Amid the turmoil, who, Sminthos, was going to notice a minuscule creature shivering at the feet of the foul horse? I had not thought battle would be like this. Quite suddenly, in the firelight, I picked out Pyrrhus again, spattered with blood and gore. He seemed to be looking right at me but this must have been an illusion because he turned abruptly and stood motionless, legs apart, staring at the temple. There seemed to be a space around him as he stood there, his right arm extended, blood dripping from his blade, as if not only Trojans but brother Greeks feared him. He bore no shield, this execrable boy, protected instead by the terror his absolute ruthlessness inspired. Then he began to stride towards the temple steps.

What foolish, insane, perverse instinct made me follow him, I do not know. I was drawn to him. I ran, as fast as I had ever run, I, who had known only the confined space of the horse's guts. I ran across that stricken place, dodging the feet of men, skidding through blood, till I was almost at Pyrrhus' heels. The steps were steep but few, and I kept up with him by climbing over fallen bodies strewn across them. The monumental gryphons did not daunt him. The temple guard melted away before him, though he did not so much as raise his sword. The temple gates with their eight great plates of silver, studded with brass, had been thrown open during the feasting and Pyrrhus walked calmly through, ignorant of the mouse trotting at his heels.

Once inside, however, I did what mice do. Timorous of the vast open space, I scurried to the wall and ran along it making myself as small as possible. I needn't have worried. Pyrrhus' eyes were fixed straight ahead. The floor was an immense mosaic featuring owls from every angle, owls in branches, owls in flight, owls with mice in their beaks. And pomegranates, whole, halved and quartered. The green-eyed owls and the crimson pomegranate seeds made it look as if the floor had been inlaid with jewels but Pyrrhus was not admiring the floor. At the far end of the atrium from where he was standing was a colossal statue of the goddess wearing a triple-crested helmet. At her feet was an altar of intricately carved stone. Before it were tripods which supported shallow bowls where flames were dancing. Standing at the altar, with one hand upon it was an old man in armour. In his other hand was a spear and clinging to him a boy of no more than ten. The man's armour had been made for him in his youth and now hung loosely on his shrunken frame. The spear trembled in his shivering arms, not, I thought from fear, but from age. He was a bleak figure. In the shadows behind the altar were an ancient woman hooded and cloaked and a girl with wild hair and wilder eyes.

Though the great doors stood wide open, the sound of battle was muted in here and the air sweetly wreathed with incense. It seemed oddly quiet. But the eyes of the old man did not take in the beauties of the temple, nor were they fixed on Pyrrhus, but over his shoulder at the burning city and where the hideous horse stood silhouetted in the firelight. Suddenly, the little boy broke free and rushed at Pyrrhus who felled him with one stroke, cutting through the shoulder almost to the waist.

As the child lay there in a widening pool of blood, the old man loosed a cry of such wretchedness as would have shaken Hades, and weakly threw his spear. Its weight was too much for him and it fell short by a long way, hitting the floor with a clang and sliding forward a few pointless inches. Even so, he drew his sword and held it trembling before him.

'I know who you are, filth-born. You have polluted my eyes with the murder of my child who should have lit *my* pyre. I should not have seen this crime. The gods will hunt you down for staining this most holy place with sacrilege.'

Pyrrhus laughed out loud.

'A fine speech, you festering rack of bones. Is that rusty armour all that's holding you together? You listen to this, scarecrow. I'm going to send you on a little mission. Go and tell my father, Achilles, what I have done. Go and tell him what his degenerate son is doing here in Troy. I'll give you a send-off.'

At this, I watched in awe as the High King came forward sword raised. A sorry sight. As he reached him, Pyrrhus knocked the useless weapon from his hand and it slithered on the temple floor. Then Pyrrhus held his sword behind his back, reached out and grabbed Priam's long white hair, wound it deliberately around his left hand, and dragged him, his heels slipping in his son's sticky blood, back to the altar. There, holding the king's head to the very stone, he held his flashing sword aloft in his right hand and sheathed it to the crossguard in the old man's side.

I became aware that the old woman was screaming when suddenly the girl rushed at Pyrrhus and clawed at his eyes. He struck her in the face with the fist closed around the hilt of his sword. She staggered, but reached for his face again, and laughing he punched her repeatedly till she fell to the ground unconscious. Then, he cut off Priam's head and threw it at the altar, stripped him of his armour and began dismembering the body. The old woman, ululating, turned to the wall.

Now, in a tumult of cheers, Greek soldiers, most of them Myrmidons, began to appear through the temple gates. Odysseus was among them and he stood scowling at Pyrrhus' bloody handiwork. As they all swarmed across the beautiful mosaic, Cassandra – I learnt later that that was the girl's name – began to come round. I now saw too that she was no girl but, for all her wildness, a beautiful young woman. Seeing this, Pyrrhus turned from hacking Priam's body to pieces and, leaving his butchery, signalled to his men to take her prisoner. Wiping his bloodied hands on his thighs, he began to run to one of the golden doors behind the altar, one on either side, tipping over two of the tripods as he passed. Flaming oil ran across the floor. As crazed with these horrors as the boy was with bloodlust, I ran to follow him, weirdly compelled like those spellbound travellers who are compelled to tell tales of starvation and slavery to complete strangers. As I ran, I turned to look behind me, and stumbled, rolling forward several times until I found my feet again, but I saw enough. Pyrrhus' men had bound Cassandra's wrists and they were dragging her screaming towards the temple doors. Out of the corner of my eye, I saw Odysseus moving towards Queen Hecuba, the old woman, whether to claim her as his slave or to comfort her, I didn't find out, though I doubt it was the latter.

I can only imagine traitorous spies had schooled Pyrrhus in the intricacies of the interior of the temple and its secret passageways, leading to the royal palace and who knows where else, but he ran surefootedly with me running behind him as if I had been tied to his ankles. Behind the silver doors was a narrow passage leading to a steep, stone staircase up which Pyrrhus stomped.

And there I would have been left behind, for the risers of the steps were high, but for a handrail made of blue-stained rope which ran up the right-hand side of the wall. The end of it reached to the floor ending in a golden tassel. I was able to jump onto this rope without much difficulty and scamper along it behind the impatient figure of Pyrrhus. We ran through narrow corridors which twisted suddenly at right angles several times. At first the walls were decorated with frescoes depicting the wealth of Troy with clients kings laying tribute at Priam's feet, fruit, corn, oil and wine, gold, ivory, spices and slaves. However, these soon gave way to unadorned plaster and then to roughcast as if some project had been left unfinished. The floor too had ceased to be tiled and had become rough and dusty. It was quiet in this labyrinth apart from the soft pounding of Pyrrhus' naked feet and the scratching of mine.

Another turn and the frescoes returned and the flooring was now of polished wood. Here the walls depicted Apollo slaying the Python, Apollo playing the lyre, Apollo in the golden chariot of the sun. Pyrrhus stopped, as did I. There was nowhere to run and I was done for if he turned. I realised at once why he had stopped. We could hear again the din of battle, rallying cries and the shrieks of the wounded and the dying, the harsh bray of trumpets, and the screams of panicking horses. But above it all, there was a roar which all but obliterated everything else. I have heard thunder since then, Sminthos, I have heard tumultuous seas crashing on rocks, but nothing like this raging noise.

Pyrrhus began to walk forward now and I trotted behind. Another turn and all was clear.

Or rather, all was red. We had come to a kind of enclosed bridge which I guessed must cross over a narrow street from the upper storey of the temple to one of the royal palaces. I say enclosed because it was roofed, but there were high rectangular windows on either side, through which the fire storm raged. Flurries of sparks blew across the bridge in a fiery wind and the taste of smoke was bitter on my tongue. Pyrrhus ran across it with a light tread while I paused long enough to jump onto the low ledge of one of these windows. I saw that belatedly the Trojans had rallied. The lane led to the temple precinct where a ferocious battle was being fought. Below in the constricted street, Greeks were setting up ladders against the building before us and began to swarm up them, their shields held over their heads. And they had need, for above us Trojan defenders were hurling down bricks and stones, whole gilded beams of wood of great antiquity, and whole chunks of masonry. They were desperately tearing down the very towers and turrets and pinnacles of the palace in order to defend it. A sorry paradox, Sminthos. Even a mouse could see that their wild exertions were doomed. Prodigious yellow and black flames were leaping from the ground floor windows and harrowing screams suggested women being burned alive.

I took all of this in at a glance and then I ran full tilt to catch up with Pyrrhus' flashing heels. It seemed as if, running in his wake, I had no need to fear any danger ahead, except the boy himself. The heat rising from below the bridge was indescribable. Again, once on the other side, we zigzagged through a maze of richly furnished corridors, hung with carpets and rugs in colours that seemed almost to live and writhe or adorned with shields and spears of gleaming brass. Two flights of shallow stairs, another violent twist, and Pyrrhus burst into a spacious bedchamber, all Ionian white and gold, where he stopped. A great bed lay in the centre of the chamber sumptuously carved, a white and gold-spotted antelope with ivory horns reared at each corner, and the whole beautiful, imperial thing was draped with opulent embroidered silks of purple, indigo and saffron. On one side, were eight of the same high windows which reached to the floor and through them I could see the smoke-blackened head and neck of the baleful horse which had brought me here.

For the windows looked down onto the temple forecourt. The roar and crackle of flames, acrid smoke belching into the air, bellowing and wailing and the clash of arms invaded and polluted the stately room. Fiendish firelight glowed and danced on the Parian marble and by it the room was clearly lit although there was no other illumination. Pyrrhus stood stock still where he had entered, legs apart, breathing calmly, though my heart was knocking from the run.

I saw where he was looking. Standing immobile at the last of the great windows was a young woman looking back straight at him with defiance and contempt. Despite her youth, her beauty appeared mature and inward, wholly unlike the meretricious prettiness of the painted girls I had seen through the nether eye of the horse around the Greek camp. You see, Sminthos, I had not seen much of women, though I had had more than enough of men. This one seemed, despite the obscene clamour outside, as imperturbable as the image of the goddess herself in the temple we had left behind. Her long, blue-black hair hung down her back and she wore a white, many-pleated robe, without a vestige of jewellery, though her demeanour was royal.

And now I saw with astonishment that one of her breasts was bare and that she was giving suck to a plump, healthy, naked baby, who was kneading the breast with his little hands. He seemed blissfully serene, oblivious to the apocalypse raging around him and of the callow murderer standing silently at the threshold of the room. This, I sensed, was why Pyrrhus had come across the dark sea and broken into windy Troy.

The moment seemed frozen for a long time, like a tableau in a frieze, and then Pyrrhus started forward and grabbed the little boychild – I saw it was a boy – by one ankle. Holding him high in the air in order to taunt her, he forced the woman round with the point of his sword at her throat and drove her back onto the bed. The child was squalling now and wriggling, the woman mute with shock.

'Don't move, whore, or I will carve your bastard princeling like a fat little chicken,' howled Pyrrhus. 'Stay where you are, Trojan bitch.'

And he moved to the window where she had stood, still holding the wailing child by the ankle.

'My father killed his father, shall I kill his son?'

And he held the wriggling child out through the window, high over the battle below. The woman stood appalled but dared not move, as Pyrrhus stood there, laughing at her.

I could bear it no longer. Had I come from the ships to the high citadel, for this? Had I not wanted to be a warrior? Was I not called Polemikos? I rushed forward.

But what, little Sminthos, had I hoped to do, a wretched little mouse, not much bigger than you? I think I meant to bite him on the heel, or something. As if that would have made any difference. As it was, my senseless courage evaporated as soon as I got near him, and all I did was to run across his foot, right across his toes. He dropped the child, turned in one movement, and cut off half my tail.

Oh, Sminthos, I didn't know then who that infant boy was. I still do not know if Pyrrhus would have killed the infant anyway or if my inane tickling of his foot (for that – in short – is the sum of my military exploits) had caused him to drop the wriggling little boy from that high window into the fire and slaughter way, way below, to have its brains dashed out, to be burnt, or trampled or kicked to death by horses. I still do not know if my idiotic valour was responsible for the murder of that child. And I sleep badly for it, when I sleep at all.

I had carried on running until I was crouching under the great bed. Pyrrhus had no further interest in me. The forsaken woman had rushed at him and was holding his knees screaming, as Pyrrhus' men came teeming into the room from the passage that led from the bridge. I saw, from where I skulked, Pyrrhus' men raise her from the ground and bind her wrists. She seemed to acquiesce, as it is said the antelope does when the leopard is at her throat. Pyrrhus, caked now in blood from head to foot, and none of it his, looked on, his eyes bright with lust deferred. I guessed her fate and was ashamed.

With the point of his sword, he waved the men on through another door. They left raucously, bearing the woman with them. Pyrrhus, thinking himself alone, watched the battle from the window for a while, and then was gone. I never saw him again. I was not sorry.

A mouse's tail is important to him, Sminthos, as you well know, sitting there on yours. Sitting on our tails like this is how we survey the scene, this is how we watch and listen, this is how we feed and how we clean our whiskers. It is vital to our sense of balance. It is a very sensitive organ. Shock had numbed any pain at first but now I nearly fainted at a sudden bolt of agony. I began to grimace and tears started at my eyes. There was not much blood and I curled around so that I could put the end in my mouth and suck it, much as a child might suck a cut finger. But what to do now? My short life had been pitiful and degrading enough, but now it seemed imprisoned in the fierce vexation of a nightmare.

I could not stay there. Though Pyrrhus' soldiers had moved on, the glare of fire in the tall windows and the noise of battle outside were very present threats. If I followed the soldiers, I might encounter Pyrrhus again and I was not keen on being mutilated further. There was nothing for it to go back to try and find the temple bridge.

I sensed the way without difficulty but it was foul. A thick pall of smoke hung in the narrow corridors. Crouching low, I was able to breathe, but my eyes stung, and I had to stop to sneeze often. When I reached the bridge, it was ablaze. The twisting flames revealed that for all its cunning and splendour it had been built on a wooden frame which was now just a charred black skeleton. Suddenly, after several sharp cracks, it split and fell with a roaring sigh, in an avalanche of sparks into the street below. Opposite, the sacred temple of Athene itself was on fire. As I watched, a nearby house, doubtless the palace of one of Priam's many sons, blazing at every window, sank, its three storeys collapsing with a deafening thunder. At its core was blinding white heat. Great slabs of masonry bounced along the street like toys and from under the rubble huge rolling volumes of dust and smoke and sparks seethed across the street like a tidal wave.

I looked up. If it had dawned – and surely it should have done by now? – there was no way of knowing it. Towers of filthy, billowing smoke rose up everywhere, hiding from the sun the obscene desecration of burning Troy.

For me, there was no alternative but to go back on my footsteps and to try my meagre luck on one of the passages that led off from the route Pyrrhus and I had taken earlier. I turned back into the smoke and in turning away from the direct blaze, I realised that the heat had singed my whiskers.

I made no end of false turns, retreating from passages blocked by falling roof beams, burning or smouldering in my way, by heaps of rubble, or by trapped and standing fumes, noxious even from a distance. I turned at last into a high room, cooler and quieter than anywhere I had encountered until now. It was exactly square and contained a number of elaborate dining couches with a number of little carved and inlaid tables. In the middle was a vast decorated krater for mixing wine. Along one side were four of the high windows that were a feature of the architecture of this building. The chamber must have been near the centre of the palace for it looked down into an inner courtyard surrounded by lofty sycamores and at the centre, unbelievably, a fountain was playing. Though I could still hear the muted rumble of fighting, I could also hear the spattering of water on the paving by the little pool. I had never heard anything so beautiful. I realised now that the hot air from the conflagration at the bridge had scorched my throat. I was very thirsty.

In the square of sky above, smoke vapours tumbled in a lurid light. The trees looked refreshing, though even here the leaves were covered with dust and ash. The branches reached almost into the room. Steadying myself on my haunches, I leapt for the nearest bough. I have already said that a mouse needs his tail for balance, and perhaps that is why, in my maimed state, I failed in this simple jump and failed to grasp the branch I was aiming for. I slipped, slithered and fell. Fortunately, the foliage was thick and I was light. Clutching at leaves I was able to manoeuvre myself onto a safe breathing space in a fork of the branches, and at length, when I was rested, to scramble down the bark of the tree. To my intense relief, there were broad shallow steps to the edge of the little pool where I was able to slake my thirst and soothe my parched throat in the cool water, at first in tiny sips, as birds do, then in a longer draught.

I wanted to stay here forever, but knew that the all-consuming fire was rolling surely inwards and I guessed that this little haven would soon be the site of a hideous updraught of angry flame. I searched around me in little circles and pointless darts, thinking that the fire must have fried my brain when I saw by chance a possible means of escape and realised that I was not devoid of some little strategic sense after all.

I saw that the bottom of the pool was not level but sloped downwards to one side, and that along the poolside wall where the water appeared deepest were outlet vents to drain the pool if the water rose too high. At the moment the water level was low and, in any case, the vents seemed stuffed with wet leaves. Now these outlets must lead to some sort of drainage system which might, if I were lucky, lead out of the city. Who knows, Apollo willing, I might even be sluiced out of the burning city and flushed into the River Scamander itself. If so, I told the god, I would never again aspire to be a soldier, I would change my name and live quietly and modestly in the country.

We mice can swim pretty well, Sminthos, though we rarely choose to. I can see from your face that you haven't tried it and I don't blame you. Instinctively, we use our tails whipping them from side to side and kicking with our back legs. I was not averse to getting in the water. Not only had I been subject to excruciating heat of late, but my fur was matted with dust and soot and flakes of plaster. I slipped in, not far from the vents, and, despite the handicap of an abbreviated tail, I was soon pulling away the soggy leaves with my forepaws and slithering through the vent into a downward-sloping tunnel.

At first all was well. The pipe was broader than I expected and quite dry apart from a snaking runnel of water that ran lazily downward. After a while it joined a wider channel with a gutter down the middle. This tunnel was made of brick, and as I ran down it, I saw that other pipes fed into it, perhaps leading from other pools and fountains. Even so, the stream that ran down the middle was not more than a trickle. I guessed, from its angle and disposition, that it might run under or alongside the ceremonial ramp which led up to the temple of Athene and up which the fatal horse had been dragged.

On I ran, delirious with hope, holding what remained of my tail high and barely aware of its throbbing. Despite my exhaustion, I kept up a steady pace for I was young and focused on freedom and it seemed within my grasp. The tunnel opened wider and wider until a man could have crawled through it and I noticed more and more pipes leading into it, sometimes just tubes of wood, but often of lead or copper. However, the sparse rivulet of water in the central channel had dried up completely.

Imperceptibly, I became aware of a rise in temperature and then of threads of vapour in the air. The tunnel suddenly dipped into a steeper incline and here what I could see pulled me up short. The threads of vapour became wafts and puffs and then clouds of steam. I could see ahead that other channels as broad and wide as this one had come together and that at the intersection the whole fabric had collapsed. Before me the way was totally blocked by brick and embers. The heat was such that the bricks had fused and molten lead ran in crazy channels down the blockage, silver at first then cooling to yellow green. What a firestorm there must be above ground to create this furnace down here.

My heart sank with disappointment and I cursed myself for being so foolish as to hope. What, in my whole wretched life, had ever happened to me that I should have allowed myself the luxury of hope? I would have to backtrack again.

Wearily, I turned back uphill. The best I could think of was to go back to where I could find a feed-pipe where water was still running, however feebly, and to try to climb it. It was a desperate plan, but I was tired and by now totally dejected. After some time, I found one which was warm but not too much so and I squeezed myself into it. To my surprise, it was not long before I emerged into a shallow well of some kind, though it had but a puddle of water in it and it was not hard to climb up its sides. I emerged, of course, into maddening noise beneath a sky where a vortex of smoke and sparks and flashes still whirled. To the racket was added a new noise, the clatter of cart wheels and cobbles.

This was not the sacred way which led from the temple to the Scaean Gate, but a narrow cobbled alley though it also rose up to the flaming citadel whose once illustrious towers were now black ruined fingers pointing accusingly at a sky on fire. Downhill was no ceremonial gateway but a little postern gate, and flowing down the gradient were crowds whose faces were running with sweat and soot. Countless grimy feet moved past me – men, women, children, beasts – and the great clattering wheels of oxcarts laden with what goods these refugees had been able to throw together at the last minute. The buildings on either side were yet intact although flames crackled in their upper storeys and blazing debris was falling everywhere,

I ran frantically up and down, clinging to the wall, trying to get my bearings. How to join these people without being noticed? For a moment there was a gap in the stream of people flowing down the hill and in the garish light I glimpsed a bizarre spectacle. A handsome man in full armour came down the hill. The armour was no common stuff – I had never seen anything so fine, and the purple plumes nodding on his helmet proclaimed him to be of the highest rank, maybe even royalty. But that was not what was strange. Over his shoulders was thrown a lion-skin and on it sat a skinny old man, enfeebled with age. Their appearance was rendered even more curious because the warrior also held the hand of a pretty lad of about eight who was clearly struggling to be brave. Behind them, but at some distance, walked a woman of rank with a fold of her robe over her head, clutching a sizeable bundle of some kind to her breast.

Just as the warrior. the old man on his shoulders. and the little boy passed me, but before the woman reached me, a brick fell and bounced in front of me and so startled me that I ran out into the middle of the street. The woman bent over her bundle, saw me, screamed, dropped it, and stopped dead. I had just time to see that the bundle contained the silver figure of a goddess wrapped in the costliest cloth of gold, before a flaming joist came hurtling down and crashed between us throwing up a frenzy of sparks. A burning coal from the beam embedded itself in the matted fur on my left haunch and burnt both fur and skin away and I screamed too. It would have been but a speck to a human but it near crippled me. I rolled over several times to put out the ember. The glare obliterated any sight of the woman. I ran or rather limped to the opposite wall and downhill, as fast as I possibly could.

The man with the strange burden turned at the crash and looked back.

'Creüsa!' he cried in anguish and then, assuming that his wife (who else could she be?) had been crushed by the beam, he turned and was borne away by the tide of people converging on the little gate.

In panic, I ran after. Just before I reached the man in armour, a wagon drawn by oxen, pulled out of a side street, laden with furniture and other household goods and stacked at the back with clothing, hangings, furs and blankets. A young family sat at the front, their eyes now fixed on the gate. With a final exertion, I leapt onto the back, and clambered onto the fabrics.

I had just time to see us pass under the lintel of the postern gate before I buried myself in the material and fell into a black and dreamless sleep.

VI

I awoke to find a breeze in my fur. I had been shaken unnoticed from the blankets and lay vulnerable in the grass. How long I had slept, I don't know, but eventually I roused myself and began to explore. I found I was part of a great company, Sminthos - men, mothers, children, and in the long waving grasses, mice. The man in armour, and his father, and his little son were there. A people gathered for exile. We sheltered on the mountain slopes, near a temple of Demeter set in a cypress grove and watched Troy burn. We were not harried by the Greeks; they were too busy plundering the houses and looting the temples.

Troy burned for many days and nights and even when the flames subsided a black plume of smoke rose to the indifferent heavens for months. Gradually, the men and woman begin to leave, the greater part of them following the man in armour with the nodding plumes.

Most of the mice remained and raised families. The sky grew blue again. It was pleasant here among the waving, silver grasses, where grasshoppers whirred and where bees droned in the wild thyme and the only heat was the heat of a bountiful sun. Plentiful seeds and insects furnished easy food. Many of the mice had been wounded more grievously than I and soon died, but the rest thrived and multiplied abundantly in the rapture of their youth.

Only I kept myself to myself, Sminthos. This easy life should have been an Elysium to me, I know, after the foetor inside the horse and the nightmare in the city, but I could not feel it. I had plenty of time to reflect on my cowardice, on the stain on my father's name, and the ridiculous travesty that is my name. Polemikos, the warrior.

No, it is not my name. It is my shame. And it is right that you should know it.

'Oh, wicked!' cried Otto, beating the ground with his front paws.

'Indeed,' replied Maximilian Emmanuel, ruefully. 'War is always wicked.'

'Nah, I don't mean that, man!'

'Please, don't address me as "man", Otto,' said Maximilian Emmanuel, gravely. 'I scorn the epithet.'

'It's just a way of talking.'

'Well, I wish you wouldn't.'

'Yeah, yeah, yeah. Don't worry about it, man,'

Maximilian Emmanuel winced.

'What did you mean?' he said.

'Well, Polemikos was a kind of hero really, wasn't he, dad?'

'There are no heroes in war, Otto. Only monsters, like Pyrrhus, and those who are unwittingly dragged into it, with silly hopes of glory and fame. Like Polemikos.'

'Virgil glorifies war.'

'He does not.'

'Who was the woman with the baby?'

'That was Andromache, the wife of Hector, and the little boy was Astyanax, Hector's son and heir. In killing him Pyrrhus destroyed the last of the royal line.'

'That bit was cool.'

'It was not my intention to make it cool,' said Maximilian Emmanuel, somewhat frostily.

'Did Polemikos really make Pyrrhus drop the baby?' asked Otto.

'Pyrrhus would have killed Astyanax anyway. That was his prime object. It was foolish of Polemikos to suppose a mere mouse could have had such an impact on history.'

'Who was the dude with the old man on his shoulders and the little boy?'

'The "dude" as you so inopportunely put it,' sniffed Maximilian Emmanuel. 'was Aeneas, as you might have guessed, the old man he was rescuing was Anchises, his father, and the little boy, Iulus, ancestor of Julius Caesar according to legend.'

'Was the woman - Creüsa, was it? – was she his wife?'

'She was. She was lost in Troy.'

'And Aeneas went on to found a dynasty that would eventually build Rome?'

'There's hope for you yet,' said Maximilian Emmanuel, licking his son's ears. 'That is indeed Virgil's claim.'

'So Polemikos did change history!' squeaked Otto excitedly. 'If he hadn't frightened Aeneas' wife, he would have been stuck with her and he wouldn't have had all his adventures and finally and ended up in Italy!' he declared triumphantly.

'Conceivably,' Maximilian Emmanuel continued cleaning his son's ears.

'I think the fire and the fighting are the best bits in Virgil,' said Otto, squirming a little.

'But, the Aeneid is fiction,' his father replied.

'Unlike your story.'

'Every word of it is true,' said his father indignantly.

'Every word may be, but the story isn't. You made it up, didn't you?'

'That is as may be,' said Maximilian Emmanuel, inscrutably. 'That is enough Latin for today. Now, what is next? You may choose, Otto: Logic or Rhetoric?'

'Whatever,' sighed Otto.

The Downing Street Cat

I

The door of Number Ten Downing Street is iconic, though I hate the term myself. It has become a meretricious floozy of a word, consorting as it does with journalists and TV presenters and other such pimps and bawds of language. It is not just a door: it is a metonym. You see, the words 'Number Ten' stand for Her Britannic Majesty's Government. That's why it is so often on the television with an iconic policeman standing in front of it looking genial - the old-fashioned sort of policeman with a pointy helmet, of course, not the paramilitary type with a yellow high visibility jacket and alarming guns.

The door is only ever opened a little way, by an unseen flunkey, to let Ministers of the Crown sidle in and out, because the common people, like you and me, or rather you, must not be allowed to see the mysteries within. The flunkey sits on a special Chippendale chair just inside the door which has a kind of leather hood to keep him from draughts. There is a two-handled drawer in the base which used to contain hot coals to warm the said flunkey's bottom. In the old days, he was probably employed because he had exceptionally keen hearing, though now he has a computer screen which tells him when someone is approaching. He takes great pride in opening the door at precisely the right moment. I sometimes wonder how you apply for such a job, and what qualifications are required. A high degree of pedantry must be among them.

It is not the original door. The original Georgian door is at the bottom of D staircase in Downing College, Cambridge. This door is quite a humble thing, not very tall really, black certainly, and edged with gold but rather battered-looking. It is the door to what is now the College Office at the stone-flagged bottom of a chilly flight of stairs. Only a gold plate marks it out from other doors in the college. But the modern door – ah, that is a door among doors. You might think it must be polished all night by invisible hands to be so lustrous and lacquered and mirror-black but that is not the case. It has got like that by being painted again and again with layer upon layer of black gloss paint. It may look as if it is made from black oak, like the original, and that its provenance from that most majestic and British of trees is part of its dignity, but that is not the case either. It is actually made from bomb-proof metal, coated with the highest quality black gloss. This has been in place since 1991 when the IRA launched a mortar attack on Number Ten from a van parked nearby.

You will never see anyone painting it, neither with visible nor with invisible hands, because there is a replica which is kept in storage. Whenever a new layer of paint is needed, usually during the summer parliamentary recess, the door is removed, by no less than eight workmen because it is exceptionally heavy, and the spare installed. Of course it looks just like a wooden door below its elegant semi-circular fanlight. It has six panels, just like the original in Downing College. The number '10' is actually painted on the door in white between the top two panels, with the nought slightly askew in deference to the original which had a clumsily affixed zero. There is a black iron knocker in the shape of a lion's head, which is just as well because the doorbell doesn't work. Nor does the letterbox.

Think about it. Why bother to cut a letterbox in a steel door when there's a flunkey to open it as soon as he sees you coming? Do try to keep up. All the same, the letter box still bears the legend, First Lord of the Treasury, which has been one of the titles of the Prime Minister for many years.

In 2006, The Daily Post reported that the door had been repainted red. Some blamed Cherie Blair and her obsession with redecoration, some blamed Teflon Tony himself and averred that it revealed his true Marxist heart, many were appalled, a few celebrated in private, but I was aware that the date was

April the First. Moreover, I don't believe anything I read in The Daily Post anyway. No, the most famous door in the world is, and must always be, very black and very, very shiny, otherwise it wouldn't be iconic, would it? Surely even you can see that.

But it is not the metonymic door which concerns me in this chronicle, rather it is the secrets which lie beyond, which you, and you alone, are privileged to hear – though I am beginning to doubt my judgement in seeking you out, I'm afraid.

Beyond the door is the entrance hall, of course. The floor is tiled in large black and white squares, like a chessboard, and there is a handsome Turkey carpet. Immediately inside the door is a set of tiny, mouse-sized pigeon holes for mobile phones. The walls are yellow, with a barely perceptible regency stripe though I believe they were pink in Mrs Thatcher's day, if you're interested in that kind of thing, which you probably are. To the right, as you enter, is a white Georgian fireplace; to the left an ornate grandfather clock; and ahead of you a portrait of Sir George Downing who built the house and the college.

However, this is all rather unimportant, and it's not really for me to give you a virtual tour, no matter how much that might titivate your voyeuristic instincts. What *is* important, and I cannot emphasise how much, is that beside the door sleeps the Downing Street Cat, Bollinger.

Now, if you were to open the iconic door, that is if the flunkey were to *let* you open it, Bollinger would be behind it. Not on the floor, you understand, oh no, that would be beneath the dignity of young Bollers. No sir, the Downing Street Cat sleeps on top of a hot air vent for hours and hours at a time with all the arrogance of his species. He doesn't give a fig that he is sleeping behind the most iconic, the most metonymic, door in the land. He is not impressed. It could be your house, or my house – though I can't abide the creatures – or anybody's house for all he cares. His sublime hauteur is not the least bit tarnished by his humble origins – Battersea Dogs and Cats Home, if you please – and he slumbers serenely in the warm updraught dreaming of nothing very taxing, for he is the laziest cat that ever retracted claws.

He is, if you like that kind of thing (and I don't), a very handsome cat, a tortoiseshell with a white bib and muzzle, white legs, and a tail ringed, rather absurdly in my view, like a racoon. Nonetheless, he is very assured in his station, perhaps conscious that his office is an ancient and venerable one, despite his rather base provenance.

Ramsey MacDonald had a cat named Rufus of England, whose food allowance was increased after the Chancellor of the Exchequer submitted a budgetary bill to parliament recommending an increase in Rufus' pay. This preposterous nonsense was debated, voted upon and passed, and Rufus thereafter became known as Treasury Bill.

Chamberlain had a cat with the soubriquet, the Munich Mouser who was, apparently, still 'in office' under Churchill. There was Humphrey, who found fame with Thatcher, remained in post under Major, and walked out six months after the Blairs moved in, though whether this was in protest at the New Labour movement or at Cherie will now never be known. Sybil's tenure under Gordon Brown was as undistinguished as her Prime Minister's, though much less damaging.

Bollinger was brought in after a large black rat sought fame by trotting past the door of Number Ten during a live BBC broadcast. The sheer chutzpah of that rat! All these wretched felines, with their names, and their historic roll of honour, are not worth a sardine compared to the superb effrontery of that rodent. Valiant rat, I salute you.

But I digress – which is foolish given your attention span. I am not concerned with the emetic sentimentality which so many humans have for *felis catus*, the domestic cat. Nor am I much concerned with the feeble follies and foibles of humans either, except for the way in which human affairs are sometimes coterminous with other more important business.

The Cabinet Room is on the same floor as the entrance hall. I don't, of course, refer to that congregation of Ministers who form HM government at all. If I were to write a record of *their* comings and goings and deliberations, divagations and tergiversations it would be a very dull affair indeed, and you probably wouldn't understand it. No, I am committed to weightier matter.

I am speaking, of course, of the real Cabinet, the Cabinet at the heart of government in the Republic of Mice which is, as I write, in session behind the skirting board of the entrance hall at Number Ten. Access, if you were permitted it, which you aren't, is via a hole chipped out of the corners where a black tile meets a white tile behind the grandfather clock. The damage was done shortly after the First World War and will not be discovered by human eyes until the clock is moved again. This clock, incidentally, is the source of the nursery rhyme, Hickory Dickory Dock, and has been ascended and descended by mice for generations at all hours of the day and night. One of them was spotted by the scribbler Rupert Brooke just before a lunch for bright young things, one hot afternoon in 1911, and he scribbled the rhyme down on his napkin after the fish course. But it is a silly thing and will detain us no longer here.

There is another hole by the jamb of that famous door, at the feet of the tireless and pedantic flunkey who watches the screen. Ironic that while he is so solicitous for the security of those who come and go through that august portal, there is considerable traffic below eye level which goes unheeded. Now, through that hole or the other, through the various dark and draughty runs behind the skirting boards, pipes, wires, ducts and conduits of that old house, even through cracks in the brickwork in the Rose Garden, they have come, the Prime Mouse and his Ministers, to discuss a matter of great moment.

Here is the roll of those assembled: There is first of all The Prime Mouse, The Rt. Hon. Sir Stuart Casparian, Bt., KG. Next in rank is the Secretary of State for Territory and Infestation, The Rt. Hon. George Milton. Then there is Leonard Small, The Secretary of State for Defence against Predation. The Secretary of State for Culture, Enlightenment and Media is Dr Joseph Jerbil and Dr Lena Breech is the Secretary of State for Reproduction and Breeding. A very distinguished mouse holds the ministerial brief for Nocturnal Affairs. He is The Rt. Hon. Sir Tom Addly, QC, KCMG. The Rt. Rev. Peter Käse is the Minister for Education.

Also present are the Minister for Foraging and Scavenging, the Minister for Rural Affairs, Burrows, Holes and Runs, the Minister for Health, the Attorney General, the Chief Whisker, and the Mouse without Portfolio.

No, I haven't forgotten the Chancellor of the Exchequer. There isn't one. What would mice want with anything so silly as an economy?

You may be wondering about these titles, such as King's Counsel and Baronet, when I have said that these very distinguished mice are the government of a republic, but you know how it is. It is hard to let go of these things. After all, the Provisional Russian Government set up its headquarters in the Tsar's Winter Palace in February 1917, admittedly after a month long looting of the wine cellars, leading to what has been called 'the greatest hangover in history'. The Louvre Palace was not razed to the ground and now belongs to the people as a museum. The French abolished the legal status of the aristocracy in 1789 and it has never been restored, yet they cling to their titles. Besides, mice are conservative in some ways and like to hoard things, bits of string, balls of fluff, paperclips, fronds of tinsel, thimbles, and titles. These last are of no intrinsic substance or value but are well-regarded trinkets. The academic titles, however, and this should go without saying, are genuine.

II

Now, I do not want you to imagine (as you probably are), a convocation of Disneyfied mice, wearing suit and tie or twinset and pearls, sitting around a miniaturised oval table on tiny little chairs, squeaking like children's toys. This is not a children's story, for heaven's sake. On the contrary, this Cabinet meeting is a frenetic affair, conducted on the move. Ministers scurry backwards and forward along the Treasury Run, making abrupt turns as policy develops, leaping over each other to gain attention, summersaulting as they gain a point, sitting back and preening whiskers to reflect when one is lost, sometimes entering a seething maul of bodies when the debate is fiercest. Occasionally, they nip and bite each other in rebuttal or dissent. And all their business is conducted in song.

Because Mice sing just like whales do. Yes, I am aware that whales are very different from mice in most respects. In point of size, certainly, and I agree that few mice tend to be ocean going-creatures on the whole, but if I am tied to your literal-minded banalities we shall never get anywhere, shall we? In point of song, a mouse is 'very like a whale', as Polonius assured Hamlet in a moment of great epistemological importance which would be beyond you. In point of song, both mice and whales have a repertoire of musical vocalisations which can transmit the expression of thoughts and emotions over considerable distances .Because mouse melody is in the ultrasonic range, human ears can no more detect their songs than they can the music of the spheres. However, I believe that human scientists in Vienna have subjected mouse song to spectroscopic analysis and come to certain limited conclusions, accurate in themselves, but woefully inadequate in their reach. They claim, for instance, that the songs of male mice are individualised, though they also contain signals of kinship. They have discovered that when slowed down, they show similarities with birdsong. What amuses me is why so-called *homo sapiens* is astonished by this? Is it not patronising? Really, as everyone knows, an elephant has more respect for mice than men do.

These boffins, or buffoons, have 'discovered' that male mice use song for wooing and that the mouse who serenades the female with the more complex melodies and subtler tonalities is more likely to seduce his intended than less gifted crooners. The very opposite of humans, then. Only a species so unobservant could have come up with this expression 'as quiet as a mouse'.

Now this is as far as the scientists have got. Mice and whales the world over are laughing their socks off.

(Yes, I know, it's just a figure of speech.)

The truth of the matter is that mice conduct their affairs through solos, duets and trios, fantasias, preludes, rhapsodies, études, sonatas, rondos, concerti grossi and symphonies of song, but also through touch and the intense sensitivity of their whiskers, and through a sense of smell of exquisite refinement. Human communication is but the babbling of toddlers by comparison. Of course, mice use song in the pursuit of sex but also, and most sublimely, for politics. And again, unlike humans, they do not mix the two. You will never encounter a sex scandal in the world of mice. Such silliness is pretty inconceivable to them anyway because they do not suffer from the puritanical neuroses which generate so much hypocritical misery in the world of bipeds.

Now, if mouse song reaches the apotheosis of its beauty and motility in political discourse, it follows that the Cabinet Meeting now in session resembles a hybrid between a rugby union match and grand opera. I sense, without surprise, that you are struggling with my helpful analogy, and I can see that if I am to get you to understand even a fraction of what is going on, I shall have to translate for you.

'And now,' says the Prime Mouse gravely, 'we come to the critical item on today's agenda. I have saved it till last in order to give it space and time for our fullest consideration. I speak, of course, of the matter of The Cat.'

A collective shudder runs through the Cabinet.

'Mr Small,' the PM addresses the Secretary of State for Defence against Predation, 'bring us up to speed.'

'Well, Sir Stuart,' says this rather large and powerful mouse, 'the situation is this. The Cat was brought in by the humans because of panic about the rat. Nobody has been bothered about the rats for years – they've come and gone, inside and out with very little trouble. They're usually so discreet. Occasionally, one of the human women glimpses one and sets up a squawking and there is talk of getting in the pest controllers but it always gets put on the back burner. Then Norman decides to let himself get caught on camera in front of 'the door' and that's that. Since Sybil went, no cat has set foot in the place. So they bring in this creature from the feline doss house.'

'Stinks the place out,' snaps Alice Sonbrun, 'riddled with pathogens.'

'We could have come to terms with that,' Leonard Small resumes, 'there would have been ways and means. After all, he seemed to be no immediate threat. He is asleep most of the time and when he isn't he is only interested in food. We've sent crack commandos to tease him into action. We've sent in assault squads on diversionary missions. We even sent in a solo volunteer to run at his food bowl, but he barely opens his eyes. We have tried collecting the poison that the humans put out for us and mixing it with his food but there is never enough and it just makes him sick up fur balls more than usual, which is pretty revolting.'

'And a health-hazard,' mutters the Minister for Health, looking up from the wires she is gnawing.

'We regularly defecate in his water bowl in the hope that he will just decamp, but nothing seems to faze him. We have even...'

'Yes, yes, yes, that's all very well, you know...' This is George Milton, Secretary of State for Territory and Infestation, a mouse of shrewdness and urbanity. 'You are not going to get rid of the thing by force. It was pointless to try. It is too big. It is too docile. It is too stupid. Open war will get you nowhere.

'All things invite
To peaceful counsels, and the settled state
Of order, how in safety best we may
Compose our present evils, with regard
Of what we are and were, dismissing quite
All thoughts of war: ye have what I advise.'

'I say, that's rather fine, George, says the Prime Mouse.'

'Paradise Lost,' snaps Joseph Gerbil, the Culture Secretary.

'Of course, it is,' says George Milton suavely. 'Did I claim it for my own? The point is that our territory is not threatened. We come and go as we please, just as we always did. The creature is too idle to concern itself with our affairs. He seems perfectly satisfied with that ridiculous toy mouse the humans have given him. He seems even to be pathetically elated that it squeaks when he pounces on it. Do you see, the hapless humans have done us a favour. There is the stench, of course, but I feel we will soon begin to get used to that. It is not much of a price to pay.'

'Well, that sounds like a cowardly and dishonourable truce to me,' says Leonard Small, as he jumps on Milton's back and bites his ear.

Squeals of outrage greet this, even from those who privately agree with Milton's policy of non-intervention. Several Cabinet members sit upright on their haunches the tips of their noses twitching in the air as if they scent an imminent reshuffle. There is much preening of whiskers and doom shudders down the length of several tails.

'Withdraw! Withdraw!' shrieks Dr Lena Breech (Secretary of State for Reproduction and Breeding) who has had several litters by George Milton and will defend him to the hilt for her children's sake.

'I think perhaps you might take the word 'cowardice' back, Leonard, old chap. We don't want to be inflammatory, you know,' says the Prime Mouse rather wearily.

'I do,' bellows the Secretary of State for Defence against Predation, insofar as a mouse can bellow.

'Perhaps we might call it 'prudence' rather than 'cowardice'?' suggests the ever-emollient Rev. Käse.

'Dereliction of duty, more like!' thunders Small. 'Abject surrender! And to what, gentlemen?...and ladies?' he adds grudgingly for he has never quite got used to female mice serving in Cabinet. 'To what? I'll tell you to what? To a CAT! That's to what!'

There ensues a din of Wagnerian proportions, a Götterdämmerung of a chorus, some shrieking 'War!' and others, rather liking the Rev. Käse's word, bawling 'Prudence'. The ruckus is seismic, but on the other side of the skirting board, you would hear nothing of this terrible music because it is pitched beyond your hearing and understanding.

The meeting of the Cabinet is now a seething knot of mice, and I am sorry to say that there is some biting and scratching going on. The cost of democracy, mice would say.

'No, no, NO!' commands the Prime Mouse, hanging somehow by one claw from a point above the run, where the rough wooden back of the skirting board meets brickwork. It has taken some scrabbling to reach this vantage point and he is covered with yellowish plaster dust and the black and sticky filaments of old spiders' webs. Despite this he retains his charisma and the assembly is silent, if not exactly still. 'Let's be absolutely clear about this. I will not tolerate this Cabinet degenerating into behaviour fit only for humans. The meeting will come to order.'

There are susurrations of shame and assent.

'We appear to have reached an impasse. War appears fruitless (a snort from Small), appeasement ignoble (a sneeze from Milton). Look, I'm a pretty straight kind of mouse, and I say the cat must go, but how? We must set up a commission...'

'Guile.'

All are surprised at the audacity of this interruption and the Cabinet is suddenly silent and still, focused on the speaker. Well, not quite, for mice are rarely entirely still: flanks shudder, noses twitch, ears gyrate, whiskers quiver and one or two of the more excitable ministers even leak a little urine at the novelty of the situation.

'I'm sorry,' says the Prime Mouse ominously, who, while he encourages debate, does not like to be interrupted.

'Guile,' says the Secretary of State for Nocturnal Affairs in the same soft, dry tone.

The Rt. Hon. Professor Sir Tom Addly, KCMG, to give him his full name and style, is a remarkable mouse, a charismatic mouse, a mouse of distinction. His birth and breeding are impeccable. He is honorary Professor of Murine Ethics at the University of Cambridge and a Fellow of Christ's College.

He received his knighthood from the Prime Mouse himself and was appointed Knight Commander of the Order of St Michael and St George for dazzling services to the state as Ambassador Extraordinary and Plenipotentiary to the City of Lincoln, though he has never set foot in the place.

He is very young to have attained all these dignities, having been born in the Rose Garden not much more than six months ago. Moreover, he is a very handsome mouse, with huge dark liquid eyes which seem to appraise you at a glance and approve or dismiss you in not very much longer. His ears are finely shaped and on the alert. His fur is sleek and beautifully groomed and much darker than is usual in his breed, almost black, in fact. His whiskers are beautiful, delicate, sensitive and artistic. His tail is dark grey, long and subtle. Only his teeth are not quite perfect. One of his incisors is a little skewed, the result of a kick-boxing incident when he was a mousling.

But it is his mind that is astonishing. It is agile and swift, razor-sharp and supremely logical. He loves to argue and debate, both on duty and off. He will cavil for hours about whether 'weird' is an appropriate word for the ancient temples of Thailand or whether 'phalanx' is a word that needs to be in every mouse's vocabulary. In chess he is scheming and ruthless. He will take himself off to eremitical crannies for long periods of secluded study and yet, when he emerges he is heartily gregarious. Females adore him and he will deign to couple with one who takes his fancy from time to time. However, he is not inclined to let relationships interfere with his work about which he is meticulous and obsessive. Many find him aloof and arrogant but this does not faze him in the least, while to the small and elect group of friends with whom he chooses to be intimate, he is unstintingly loyal. These friends find that he can be very funny.

(It occurs to me at this point that my poor obtuse reader may be wondering what on earth a mouse could know about Thai temples or Greek warfare. Has he not heard of the World Wide Web?)

If you wish to dine with him, you should know that he loves porridge but cannot stomach mushrooms.

'Guile?' says the Prime Mouse. 'What do you mean, Minister?'

'You've said yourself that we've reached an impasse,' Addly replies. 'We cannot defeat the feline through open war and an unbecoming sloth is not mouselike. However, there is a third option.'

'Guile,' says the Prime Mouse who has got where he is by passing off the ideas of others as his own.

'Precisely.'

'Do you have a plan?'

'No, Prime Mouse, I do not. But I shall have one by the end of the day.'

The Prime Mouse's whiskers twitch. His ears are laid back, his body stiffens, and he raps his tail on the ground, sure signs of irritation in a mouse. He trusts Addly. Indeed they are close friends but these enigmatic pronouncements are frustrating in the extreme. Furthermore, they divert attention away from him and towards the young minister, which he is not inclined to tolerate.

'Then you will dine with me this evening and I shall expect to hear it. Now, is there any other business?' says the Prime Mouse to the assembled Cabinet.

There is plenty of other business but Sir Stuart is disinclined to give it much of an airing. He is tired and this business of the damned cat has riled him. Never has he known such wrangling in Cabinet before and he won't have it. He dismisses the whole lot of them and they scurry off in various directions, in pairs, in groups and in factions. The last to leave is the Minister for Nocturnal Affairs who, with a minuscule tilt of the whiskers and a discreet whisk of the tail, which it is impossible to describe or appreciate unless you are a mouse, he salutes the Premier. It is a gesture of great delicacy and urbanity such as you might expect from one who has served in the diplomatic corps. Then he patters off to one of his obscure assignations.

Left alone with the burdens of office, Sir Stuart sits up on his haunches and begins to groom himself scrupulously, starting with his nose and then behind his ears, with tiny pink paws that look like miniature human hands.

Soon he feels much better.

III

At about three in the morning, he and the Minister for Nocturnal Affairs meet for dinner. They are in the great kitchen in the basement. During the day it is intensely busy and the mice stay clear of it. Now the huge, vaulted space – two storeys high - is deserted. There is an immense arched window at one end which takes up almost the entirety of one wall. Nevertheless, it is dark but for the diffuse orange sheen of a sodium street lamp in the window from somewhere above and the eerie light of the ultraviolet fly traps, where from time to time a hapless insect meets a sizzling end. Down the centre of the vast room is a chopping board table, fourteen feet long, three feet wide and as thick as a butcher's hand.

There is much polished tile and stainless steel and beechwood scrubbed almost white. To a human eye it is spotless, immaculately, astringently clean. It has to be, for this kitchen has served food to the greatest of the great in the world of human affairs, even – whisper it softly – to Her Majesty herself. Imagine the disgrace if she, or some other head of state, or a rock star, or some other dignitary or celebrity of your world, were to come down with food poisoning after passing through that iconic door. Think what the press would make of that.

To a mouse, of course, all the scrubbing and scouring, and the buffing and polishing are beside the point. Our two august ministers of Mousedom have dined excellently on spilt couscous and on green pepper stalks and their hot white seeds by the bins outside, where the council operatives have been less scrupulous about tidying up after themselves than the kitchen staff are obliged to be. Now, without recourse to security key pads and PIN numbers, the mice slide under the kitchen door with ease (no wonder the fat and dimpled sauté chef complains of drafts round his ankles) and come into the gloom for dessert, which they are sure to find, for the most scrupulous pursuit of hygiene cannot eradicate human error. A brief reconnoitre of the terrain reveals that pressed into the juncture between a cupboard and the floor is a choice quantity of caraway seeds and even some candied peel kicked there by some apprentice pastry chef too lazy or too busy to clean it up and missed by the vigorous brush and the avenging mop.

Replete, they yawn and set about grooming first themselves and then each other with their teeth and claws, first scratching themselves all over with their hind feet, then washing their faces and fur with their hands, and finally nibbling socially at each other's fur.

'Now then, Tom,' says the Prime Mouse at last. 'What's the plan? Have you got it?'

'I have,' says the Minister.

'Good,' the PM beams, touching the other's nose with the tip of his own. 'Because, you know, if I were it to leave it up to Milton and Small, the deuced cat would have bally kittens before they came up with anything.'

Professor Sir Tom refrains from pointing out that since Bollinger is a solitary male this would be anatomically unlikely. Sir Stuart does not like to be contradicted or finessed. Addly says nothing.

'Well?'

'Well what, Prime Mouse?'

'Well what? Well, what, Prime Mouse? Don't be so bloody cryptic! And don't be so bloody formal either, Tom Addly! I've known you since you were a tiny pink blind hairless COMMA! What, in the name of Mickey Blistering Mouse, IS THE PLAN?'

'Ah, the plan,' says Sir Tom maddeningly. 'That's just it, you see.'

'I don't see!' roars the Prime Mouse, suddenly grabbing his Minister with both hands and biting his fur. Sir Tom squeaks in discomfort. 'Don't play games, Tom. *What* is just it?'

'I do have a plan, Stuart, but unfortunately, I can't tell you what it is.'

'But I'm the Prime Mouse. I have to know. I demand to know.'

'That is also just it. *Because* you are the Prime Mouse, it is better that you don't know.'

'Oh, stuff and nonsense, Tom. We're old friends. You can tell me anything. You know that.'

'No, seriously, Stuart. This involves the internet and the press. It is better if you keep right out of it. Your reputation must be preserved at all costs and this is going to get dirty. Fur and feathers are going to fly when the faeces hits the fan.'

'I commend your facility with alliteration, Tom,' says the PM wryly. 'But this is all very irregular, you know. I'm not sure I can let you go ahead with this.'

'It has to be irregular. Or it won't work,' Sir Tom replies.' Moreover, Stuart, not only am I *not* going to tell you what I am going to do but you need to give me carte blanche to do it.'

'Is that really necessary?' mutters the PM sheepishly. (Yes, a mouse can be sheepish. Don't interrupt.)

'Yes, Stuart, it is.'

'Oh, very well,' says the PM. 'I say, do you fancy a game of catch?''

'I think that would be capital,' says the Minister for Nocturnal Affairs. And they work off their dinner by chasing each other round and round the gleaming kitchen floor for very nearly an hour.

IV

You will be wondering how on earth a mouse can access the internet. And I am going to tell you despite your rather dull scepticism and your poverty of imagination. Take that business about 'sheepish' just now. How sad. Look, if a human can be 'sheepish', why can't a mouse? It's not difficult really. Oh, never mind. I can see I've lost you.

Now, compared with the White House or the Élysée Palace, Ten Downing Street may seem rather domestic, no more than a smart town house tucked away from the testy, roaring, blaring traffic of Whitehall. It is discreetly unassuming. It tells the world that it has no need of ostentation and that it is at ease with itself. The iconic Georgian door murmurs to the world that within, over tea and hot buttery pikelets, sage heads are inclined over richly embossed documents. They mean to secure the destiny of the Empire, even though it no longer exists.

The truth is, of course, quite different and the gentility a façade. Number Ten is the dazzling hub of the most sophisticated, state of the art technologies. Data pulses like life blood along fibre optic arteries, streams through cyberspace, and rolls and tumbles in clouds dense with fiscal thunder and charged with diplomatic lightning. The traffic is incessant. Emails rocket back and forth. The Twittersphere is as noisy and agitated as an aviary of finches. Inboxes swell with messages, press releases, memoranda, commands, exhortations, prohibitions. Much information is protected with intricate codes and protocols but most is public and proliferating. PC screens shimmer with charts, graphs and animations. On every surface - desks, tables, chairs, sofas and shelves - lie iPhones, iPads and other tablets, Blackberries, Androids and laptops, humming and bubbling with the transaction of info. Uploading and downloading round the clock.

Sir Tom Addly, or Tom as I shall call him, for I know him well, is very familiar with all this. Indeed he is an internet adept. He acquired several email addresses when he was a very young mouse and his address book is chock-full of contacts with politically and technologically minded mice the world over. His most prolific correspondence is with an elderly and very learned mouse in Lincolnshire, whom he regards as his mentor and from whom he has received trenchant advice in the matter of The Cat.

Tom's ultimate target is the Downing Street Press Office, but there is no way he can achieve what is needful directly. The Press Office is active 24/7, to use that deplorable but indispensable expression. He has inspected it often from one of the many vents where ropes and loops and coils of wiring run from the servers to batteries of computers which are, to mix my metaphors as politicians are apt to do, the real levers of power in the land. Indeed, it was this conduit of cables which first helped him to creep into the little warren of rooms which are the engine of government publicity. Tom needs to access and harness that power.

He has watched harassed young men in shirtsleeves and tousle-headed girls with ardent lipstick and flashing nails sit on each other's desks and argue amid a litter of paper cups and pizza boxes. The men are sweaty with ambition and the girls hard-faced with the lust for a scoop. He has observed them closely. He has learned their names. He knows what makes them tick. Tom will need to divert their drive to his own purposes, but not directly, not here. First of all, he must prepare the bait.

Tom's nocturnal explorations have been extensive. Unlike many mice who are content to spend all of their lives in the runs between a couple of rooms, Tom knows the house intimately, and much of Number Eleven too. He knows that, curiously, the best bet on finding what he needs is in the flat at the top of the house where the human PM lives with his family. It is the Premier's habit, when it is time to go to bed, to leave his iPad lying on the sofa in the kitchen of the Downing Street flat.

A little out of breath as a result of the arduous climb up through the house, via pipes and wiring, through ducts, up heavy brocaded curtains, and along the grimy mazes behind the skirting board, Tom emerges from a minute hole behind the trendy black bookcase furnished with cookbooks and patters towards the equally trendy lemon sofa. He scoots effortlessly up the side. And there it is, screen facing upwards and on standby. Almost casually, he taps the home button with his foot and the screen is illuminated casting an eerie blue glow into the kitchen. It is reflected in the immaculate white walls, the spotless aluminium pots and pans and the flawless Dartington glassware. The blue screen with its seascape is also reflected in the black screen of the television, just by the sofa.

Recovered now from his climb, Tom begins to dance. Suavely, he slides one foot to the right to unlock the tablet's awesome power. The icons for various apps appear. He hops onto the icon which summons up a search engine, slides a foot again to bring up the keyboard and in no time at all has set himself up with a Facebook account and a Twitter account. Of course, he has to lie about his age because he is not over thirteen. In fact he's only six months old, but who's to know? A random name generator app supplies him with the rather distinguished user name, Inigo Vernon, and he cannot resist the password 'dangermouse1789', though he's slightly ashamed of it. A quick trawl through Google images supplies a portrait of a nerdy looking youth with spiky red hair and inch thick specs which becomes Inigo's profile picture.

Could you but see Sir Tom, my dear but limited reader, you would have been enthralled. Hours of practice over many, many nights have lent him a sureness of foot on the QWERTY keyboard. Watch him dancing rapidly over the most used keys to the left of the keyboard, and then leaping with grace and agility from the A to the P or the L to the W, with every so often an assertive stamp on the space bar. You can see his text oozing mellifluously onto the screen as he creates his fictitious autobiography: Studied at St John's College, Cambridge and Michigan State University School of Journalism. Member of the political party currently in government. Male. Interested in women. Employed as computer analyst. Freelances as a journalist. Tom puts the bait meticulously on his hook. Likes Dubstep, Metal, Lola Lo, Nietzsche, Herman Hesse, J.R.R. Tolkein, Margaret Thatcher, Catch 22, Catcher in the Rye, HIGNFY, Scrubs, Topgun, 300, Troy, Skyrim. Beach volleyball. Supports Chelsea FC. Favourite quotation: 'God is dead.' Religious views: Jedi.

He is aware that this eclectic mix is hardly a coherent character, but, for one thing, humans are not very coherent anyway (you're not, are you?), and for another, that is not the point. The point is to make as many Facebook friends as quickly as possible in order to add credibility to his account. Therefore the net needs to be cast quite wide. He puts a wildly enthusiastic review of a certain metal band into his status and gets a couple of likes almost immediately. He types in 'So it begins...' and gets several more. He makes some reactionary comments on current political affairs and gets an avalanche. Gleefully, he sends friend requests to all these names and is quickly added by most. He checks out his friends' friends and sends requests to them, sometimes with a flattering, cajoling message, sometimes with a cheeky provocation. He seeks out pictures of girls with lopsided haystack hair, ample breasts, orange triangular faces, clownish make-up and eyelashes that look like spiders and tells them, 'you look really gorgeous, babez.' They write 'aaaawwwwww! thanks,hun. what he said', and add him. He expresses his intention of visiting a number of rock festivals and enquires openly about the availability of weed. He is met with a chorus of 'YOLO!' and his street cred burgeons. He leaks a lot of totally fictitious political innuendo, gossip and surmise about some very senior figures in the human government and hints that he is placed to furnish more.

Thin dawn light begins to leak through the curtains and he can hear children stirring in a nearby bedroom. His last move is to link his Facebook and Twitter accounts and to sign out of both. He has a hundred and forty-seven FB friends and nearly as many Twitter followers. He is richly satisfied with his night's work but utterly exhausted. He has been dancing for hours, after all, and plans to sleep the bright day away behind the black bookcase. He has just enough energy to power off the iPad and leap to safety as a door opens and a small boy walks into the room.

V

On succeeding nights, he continues his clandestine work on whatever electronic device he can find. Within ten days, he has acquired 1,236 friends and a number of followers on Twitter who are rated as celebrities. You want to know who they are, don't you? Haven't you heard of injunctions? My lips are sealed.

On the eleventh night, the bait is taken. There is a friend request from a Martin 'Fractal' Spellar. (Oh, that nerdy 'Fractal'! How Tom sniggers! It is quite perfect.) The Minister for Nocturnal Affairs closes his beautiful eyes in blissful self-satisfaction. Martin is one of the harassed, perspiring, shirt-sleeved young men in the press office – the one with the flourishing and very shiny zit in the wing of his nose. With a nonchalant tap of his forepaw, Tom adds him.

VI

The next evening sees Tom and the Prime Mouse sharing breakfast in a herbaceous border in the gardens which stretch in an L-shape along the back of numbers 10 and 11. The Prime Minister's children have each planted a sunflower and are competing to see whose grows tallest. This is of no interest to the mice. They are eating the seeds.

'Now look, here, Tom,' says the Prime Mouse when they are sated.

'Where?' says Tom.

'What?' says the PM.

'Look where?' says Tom.

'Eh?' splutters his leader, non-plussed. Then he realises he is being joshed. 'Oh. Now don't be facetious, Tom. What I want to know is what you are doing about the cat. Nearly a fortnight gone and nothing done. What do you have to say?'

'I have to say that a great deal of progress has been made,' says Tom. 'These things take time you know.'

'How *much* time, dammit?' The PM is quivering with frustration from the tip of his aristocratic nose to the very end of his magisterial tail.

'Can't say.'

'You really are the most exasperating mouse that ever grew whiskers.'

'Let's just say that the time to light the blue touch paper and retire is not far off.' Tom begins to groom himself suavely.

'*How* far off?'

'Dunno.'

The Rt. Hon. Sir Stuart Casparian, (Bt., KG) approaches Tom and begins to box him gently about the ears. Laughing, Tom turns, kicks out with both hind legs, knocking the PM onto his back, and races off into a shrubbery.

VII

I hope you are keeping up, because you'll need to. Things begin to move very fast from now on.

Deftly, Tom begins to feed Martin 'Fractal' Spellar nuggets of gossip about life in Number Ten which are wholly fabricated, not worth rebutting, but slightly juicy nonetheless. Martin asks how Tom knows what the Prime Minister's wife wears at the breakfast table, what her nickname for him is (Buttercup), why the Chancellor of the Exchequer wears odd socks; how he knows about the Deputy Prime Minister's body odour, the contents of the spacious attics, the menu for state banquets, what the gardeners are paid, how greedy the Foreign Secretary is, how much the PM's wife spends on nail varnish, how the Home Secretary smokes forty Rothmans a day (mostly in the Rose Garden) and how utterly, unreservedly and irrefutably useless Bollinger, the Downing Street cat is; how Number Ten is over-run with mice while the pampered cat looks on. Tom says that he cannot reveal his sources or they will be compromised. Martin says that's fine, just keep this stuff coming, and only keep it exclusive to him. Martin will find a way of making it worth Inigo's while. Tom assents and they swear each other to secrecy.

Tom rolls onto his back and scrabbles at the air with all four legs in jubilation.

Imagine then his glee when his feeds begin to appear as little boxed stories and fillers in the redtop tabloids. Tom knows this because Martin emails a screen capture of each of his leaks to him. The first appears in The Orb, the most sensationalist and popular of them all.

PREMIER'S WIFE LIVES EXCLUSIVELY ON CELERY

Sarah Brant-Broughton, wife of the Prime Minister, just eats celery when off duty, the Orb can report. At state functions and when dining out with him or with friends, she eats just like everyone else. 'How do you think she keeps her gorgeous figure? She's so self-disciplined,' Annabelle Norton D'Isney told us. Sarah is the daughter of the seventh Earl of Stragglethorpe.

Shortly after the appearance of this little gem, Tom/Inigo receives friend requests on Facebook from Jacintha McQueen, Primrose Marsh, Jüri Metcalf-Slovo, and Daniel Deronda. Wonderful! These are more of the shirt-sleeved young men and the hard-faced girls who work in the press-office. But Tom does not accept their requests. He has no need of them from now on. In fact, he de-activates his Facebook and Twitter accounts. He and Fractal will communicate only by email now.

The leaks begin to appear more frequently, most often in The Orb, but occasionally in The Daily Post, and The Daily Mercury, two middle ranking papers, representing the middle-aged, middle-class, middle-income, small minded people of middle England. Amongst the more diverting of these squibs you might want to look up the following:

NUNS STORM NUMBER TEN (Orb)
PM WEARS SOCK SUSPENDERS (Orb)
FULL BOTTLES OF FINE WINE FOUND IN NUMBER 10 BINS (Post)
DEPUTY PM THROWS UP IN CABINET (Mercury)
WODGE OF PM'S HEADED NOTEPAPER FOUND IN PUB LOO (Orb)

PM SELLS USED TOOTHBRUSH FOR CHARITY (Orb)

SARAH BB TO RUN BBC? (Post)

And then, before too long, Tom strikes gold. Quite a lengthy patch on page four of The Orb:

CAT-ASTROPHE!

Bollinger the Number 10 cat is 'no bolly good'

The Downing Street cat is 'not fit for purpose', a government source told The Orb today. 'He does nothing but sleep and he's getting fat with it.'

Bollinger, a large tortoiseshell cat with a white bib and socks, was brought in from Battersea Dogs and Cats Home to wage war on rodents when a large black rat was caught on television scurrying past during a live broadcast from outside Number Ten. He was said to be a ruthless and successful hunter.

'I don't know who wrote his reference,' said our source, 'but it's b******s. He sleeps on top of a hot air vent all the time and only gets down to eat. Sarah (the Prime Minister's wife) feeds him on smoked salmon, would you believe it?

'Actually, the big problem in this place is not rats, but mice. I expect they come out at night and laugh at him. I can't see him staying in the job much longer.'

Should Bolly be sacked in this cat and mouse game? Yes or No? Vote in our Orb-ilicious poll on Page Six of your fun-packed paper today. We'll send the results direct to the PM.

Tom is exceedingly pleased with that last touch. It came to him after a particularly satisfactory liaison with a female behind an ormolu clock on the mantelpiece of the yellow drawing room.

VIII

Stories about the uselessness of the Downing Street Cat begin to proliferate in the tabloids. The Red Flag, the only really left-wing paper around anymore, claims that Bollinger has turned his back on his humble origins and has become a pampered lackey of the capitalist élite. Protests from animal lovers swell the letters pages of the other rags. Tom is always pleased with himself but his self-satisfaction at these developments exceeds the bounds of narcissism. He hardly needs to feed Fractal with bait at all now. This story will run and run.

The Orb publishes the results of its poll. 59% say the cat must be dismissed, 24% think he should stay, 17% don't know.

THE PEOPLE HAVE SPOKEN, trumpets The Orb, BOLLY MUST GO!

The Post sides with The Orb and bellows: SHOW THE CAT THE DOOR! alongside a picture of the iconic portal with which I began this account. There is even a little cartoon of the door slightly open to reveal an enormous boot with PM written on it which has propelled an obese and rather startled cat into Downing Street.

The Mercury, as always, decides to take a contrary position to The Post. It runs: A CAT IS FOR LIFE SAYS PRIME MINISTER'S WIFE.

PM IN CAT FLAP is the Post's riposte.

Tom is especially pleased when the controversy features for the first time in a 'quality' paper with P45 FOR FAT CAT? This is The Custodian, a pinko broadsheet favoured by the chatterati.

One night, Tom takes the Prime Mouse up to the flat and shows him all the emails in which Fractal has relayed this press activity.

'Well, yes, Tom, my dear fellow,' he says, 'this is all very well and exceedingly droll, I don't doubt, but the fact of the matter is that the bloated beast is still here, and stinking the place out. It is quite unendurable. And all you've been doing is playing games. I'm disappointed in you, Tom, I really am. Now, I'm sorry to have to say this, vieux haricot, but I've been thinking of a reshuffle and …'

'Oh, TOSH!' says Tom.

Sir Stuart's tail goes bolt upright in outrage.

'What did you just say?' he growls.

(No, you're right. Mice don't growl. But I'm translating for you, aren't I? And that is as near as I can get.)

'I said "TOSH!" – tosh, twaddle and tripe! Do try not to be so pompous, Stuart. Of course this operation will not get rid of the cat in itself. Did I ever say it would? This is skirmishing, softening the ground, recruiting allies, trading intelligence, a purely preparatory phase of the conflict. Now is the time for action. Prime Mouse, your finest hour approaches. Call the Cabinet.'

'What?'

Sir Tom Addly takes his very fine tail in both tiny hands and begins to stroke it luxuriously.

'Stuart, I am starting to worry about you. Are you sure you're not going deaf? I said: "Call the Cabinet".' And he streaks off and disappears under the kitchen door.

Sir Stuart Casparian is flabbergasted. Why does he let this youngster, barely out of its nest, bully him so? The answer is, he supposes, that he has nourished this prodigy and brought him on, and that he is immensely proud of him. One day, however, though perhaps not just yet, he must be taught some manners.

He takes a leisurely if labyrinthine route back to the Treasury Run where he lifts the tip of his nose in the air and, whiskers quivering, sets up a ululation of pulsating intensity. If you could hear it – which you can't, because it's ultrasonic (I told you that) – it would be somewhere between Susan Boyle and an air raid siren.

And sure enough, in ones and twos, the Cabinet begins to arrive.

IX

'Ladies and Gentlemen, I expect you are wondering, as well you might, why I have called this emergency meeting of Cabinet. You may have resigned yourselves to thinking that we don't have a cat in hell's chance of getting rid of Bollinger (if you'll pardon the expression), but I tell you, our finest hour approaches. I hand you over to the Minister for Nocturnal Affairs, who will reveal all to you.'

He sticks his wet nose quite literally into Tom's left ear and whispers: 'This had better be good.'

It *is* good. Tom explains what he has been up to, how he has raised the Press to such a pitch of sensitivity and curiosity that they are desperate for a scoop. They, the mice of Number Ten Downing Street, must give the fourth estate a story so compelling that it will be remembered in the nation's history for all time. This time the story must be fact, not fiction.

There is not the usual ruck and maul at this meeting. Ministers listen attentively, grooming themselves and each other. Tom continues.

The time of appeasement is over, he tells them. He sings to them passionately.

'The time for reconnoitre, for intelligence gathering, for strategic planning is past. Guile has done its work. Now is the time for action! Mice of Destiny, my counsel is for open war!'

The Cabinet goes berserk. The Ministers become a seething coil of enthusiasm, clambering over each other's bodies, nipping each other in excitement, and squeaking so audibly that a maid passing through the entrance hall pauses for a moment to wonder if she is hearing things. Only George Milton sits apart from the mêlée, looking reflective.

Tom calls them to order.

'Leonard,' Tom addresses the Secretary of State for Defence against Predation. 'You must take command. We will need not only the Cabinet, not only the Praetorian Guard, not only the army, but every single mouse in the house. We shall cover ourselves in glory.'

The Prime Mouse gazes at his protégé in stark adulation.

'Now, this is the plan,' continues the Minister for Nocturnal Affairs. 'Tomorrow, Richard Brant-Broughton, Her Majesty's Prime Minister and First Lord of the Treasury, will receive The President of the United States of America, here at Downing Street. There will of course be a banquet…

X

Compared with the seats of government in other wealthy countries, Downing Street is really pretty modest. The state dining room, however, is not. It is opulent in a confident, majestic, eighteenth-century sort of way. Facing you as you enter through the double doors is a vast portrait of George II looking wonderfully pompous in white stockings and ermine-trimmed coronation robes. There is a white vaulted ceiling with decorated ribs from which depends a many-branched golden candelabrum on a golden chain. Illumination is also provided by sconces on the rich oak-panelled walls. Along one wall are three high windows with sumptuous cream drapes and on the facing wall there are tall mirrors whose frames have an imperial Roman theme. Beneath them are a number of ornate sideboards.

Tonight, the usual highly-polished walnut table with its twenty Adam style chairs has been removed and other tables brought in to accommodate all the Very Important Persons who will be attending the banquet in honour of the President. These tables are set out in an elongated horseshoe and covered with spotlessly white Irish linen tablecloths. At each place setting there are two starched napkins laid across each other to form a star shape. The crockery gleams. There is an abundance of sparkling cutlery, predicting many courses. At intervals along the tables are silver, four-branched candelabra and at each end of the top table there are two large silver epergnes piled high with glistening black grapes. The centrepiece of the top table is a glorious flower arrangement of red, white and blue roses, representing the colours of the union flag and the stars and stripes. The blue roses are strange and ravishing. They have been flown in at great expense from a nursery in France where they are created by injecting a blue dye into the bark of the roots, a technique perfected in Arabia in the Twelfth Century.

All this magnificence stands on an enormous Turkey carpet of dark crimson, blue and gold, and across this luxurious expanse, Leonard Small and Sir Tom Addly are watching from behind one of the Queen Anne legs of a sideboard.

The candles are lit. At first the flames fizz, tremble and waver and then stand brightly upright, as do the white-gloved flunkys who line three walls behind the tables. It is quiet.

The double doors are thrown open and a buzz of conversation rushes into the room. Here they come, some of the most important people in the world.

Of course, the mice, and believe me, there are more than two, see only feet at first. The first pair are those of Richard Brant-Broughton, the Prime Minister, patent leather dress shoes as shiny as treacle. Beside them and below the hem of an evening gown in scarlet crepe de chine are the ivory and pearl Christian Louboutin high-heeled shoes of the first lady of the USA. Then comes another pair of patent leather shoes, those of Mr President himself, and beside them, elegant, understated, almost casual, white satin slingbacks below a many-pleated gown in turquoise silk. This, of course, is the fragrant Sarah Brant-Broughton, who knows the difference between style and ostentation.

And in they come, more and more shoes, the men's very much the same, apart from an Arabian robe in white, edged with gold, and a cardinal's red soutane. The ladies' shoes arrive in all manner of hues and sizes and shapes much like their ankles: some so beautifully turned that even a mouse might want to kiss them, some varicosed and puffy, one with a rather radically tattoo of a bee and a scorpion stinging each other, and one with an angry insect bite which could ruin her dinner.

But these are not the feet Tom is looking for. An unprecedented doubt seizes him. What if he has it all wrong?

Suddenly, the chatter ceases. The feet are standing behind the feet of the chairs. The cardinal says a short, ecumenical grace in a North Country accent, a trite thing which lacks any grace at all, and immediately the roar of conversation resumes along with the shifting of chairs and the seating of the ladies. Glasses are filled by the flunkeys: choice wines, red, white and Portuguese green, but no food is served yet. The double doors open again and more feet arrive, about fifteen pairs, and they shuffle in to form a line along the wall where the windows are.

Tom relaxes. 'And did those feet...?' he hums to himself.

For these feet, or at least the shoes, are very different. There are a couple of pairs of brown ones, a pair of suede ones, a pair of desert boots, a pair of Doc Martens, and the rest are trainers. They are all scuffed and grubby and even from the other side of the room Tom's finely attuned nostrils catch a rather disagreeable tang.

'Two minutes, gentlemen. No more,' says Richard Brant-Broughton in his famous baritone which sounds like rich tea biscuits dipped into hot chocolate. 'Just carry on as normal everyone,' he says. 'These guys don't like posed photographs, do you? OK then, come on, chaps, let's get it over with.'

Even you will have worked out that this is the Press corps, allowed a very brief photo-shoot before being bundled out. They raise their Nikons and their Canons.

'Now,' Tom whispers in his general's pink-lined ear.

'NOW!' sings out, Leonard Small, Commander-in-Chief of the Murine Expeditionary Force, and this vast, ultrasonic single note is somewhere in between the exultant bellow of a blue whale breaching the waves in the South Pacific and Placido Domingo performing at Wembley Stadium.

The response is instantaneous.

Four hundred and eleven mice rush onto the carpet. They come from holes between the skirting board and the floor so tiny that even the cleaners have never noticed. They squeeze en masse from under the double doors where they have been waiting in the anteroom. They slide down the drapes after hiding all day in the pelmets. They ooze from gaps in the oak-panelling too narrow and fine for humans to remark. One even appears through a hole you might have thought to be a knot in the wood. They come from behind the Roman style mirrors and the portraits of long-dead grandees. They come from behind the sideboards and the plinths on which stand bronze, neo-classical urns.

They are at first like the incoming tide on a shallow beach. Within seconds they are a tsunami. They are not in organised squadrons, battalions or phalanxes. They flush around the carpet in surges and eddies in reckless excitement. It was Leonard Small who led them out, but it is the Prime Mouse who is in their midst now, rapturously singing an ultrasonic battle-song at Wagnerian volume.

It is the amply upholstered wife of a civil service mandarin who sees them first. She stands, screams and points.

(No, she doesn't stand on a chair. Please don't urge such asinine clichés on me.)

The other ladies follow the direction in which her finger is pointing and scream too, standing and gathering their skirts about them. The cardinal and the Arabian prince follow suit. The men stand and chairs crash. Wine glasses topple and fall. The hitherto impassive flunkeys step forward helplessly.

Now, I hope, dear reader, that you don't suffer from epilepsy as well as a dearth of imagination. I should have warned you that this story contains flash photography.

For, the cameras snap, crackle and pop, click and whirr, and detonate like sheet lightning across the room.

Armed security guards crash into the room.

'Get rid of them!' shouts Richard Brant-Broughton, pointing at the photographers, who are bundled unceremoniously out of the room and out of the house. The guards, who have no idea what is going on, have not the wit to seize their cameras.

'Get rid of them!' screeches Sarah BB, pointing at the mice, or rather, pointing at the carpet, because all the mice have gone.

They have disappeared as quickly as they appeared, if not more so. Tom has warned them that the charge would be dangerous, if exhilarating, but none of them must risk their lives. After all, a good many of them are little more than pups. Once the screaming starts, he has told them, and the cameras begin flashing, they must make a precipitate retreat whence they came without any silly bids for glory. They have obeyed him to a mouse.

The whole operation has lasted no more than sixteen seconds.

During this time, Tom has not joined the fracas, though he has watched, his flanks shuddering with lust for battle. He is no coward, but he must reserve himself to witness its final scene, without which all this would be completely meaningless.

With the ejection of the press, the room has fallen silent. The President stands, arms akimbo. The First Lady has moved from her place next to the Prime Minister and is clutching his right arm for support, with her head on his shoulder. Sarah BB has sat down again and is slumped over the table, silently sobbing. The guests are all looking at the top table waiting for a reaction.

The tableau does not hold for long. The Premier, who everyone can see is trembling with rage, smites the table, excuses himself to the President and his wife, and to the rest of the table, and strides down the room on the window side, scattering flunkeys as he goes. He marches through the double doors towards the top of the stairs which lead from the first floor down to the corridor beyond the entrance hall. The staircase wall is adorned with portraits of former premiers.

Richard Brant-Broughton, your portrait will be joining them sooner than you think.

Tom immediately squeezes under the skirting board, follows a run through to the outer wall of the building, slithers down a chute he prepared some time ago by chewing through the cavity wall insulation, follows another brief tunnel at breakneck speed, and emerges from behind the grandfather clock in the entrance hall, just as the Prime Minister bursts onto the black and white tiles. Tom can see what he is looking at and knows why his face is contorted with fury.

Serenely oblivious, Bollinger, the Downing Street Cat, is blithely sleeping on top of the hot air vent.

XI

The next morning, the cat has gone. I expect you would like some kind of sentimental drivel about his going to a good home and all that, but mice are not sentimental, so you'll have to make it up for yourself, if you can.

Tom waits behind the clock and watches the Prime Minister take out a mobile phone, bark out a few commands and march off. An hour later a man in uniform is admitted through the black door and grabs hold of Bollinger who tries to scratch him, but he is not fully awake, and before he knows it he has been stuffed unceremoniously into a wicker cat basket and the man in uniform departs.

Tom yawns with satisfaction. He slips through a convenient hole and disappears down a run in which, just around a corner, he has already prepared a nest of shredded newsprint which he filched earlier from a paper abandoned by the porter's leather-backed chair. A strip chewed off from The Orb, as it happens. He does not even bother reporting to the Prime Mouse and sleeps for many hours.

It is not until the evening, when he checks his emails from Fractal, that he sees, unsurprised, what a wonderful time the press have had with the story. It seems that the Prime Minister acted very quickly, moved all the guests out into the Rose Garden, where, since it was a balmy evening, chairs were set out, lanterns lit, tables brought, and the magnificent dinner served up as a kind of improvised buffet. A posed photograph of the PM and the President beaming and shaking hands is splashed across all the papers, not only the tabloids and The Custodian, but also the rather stuffy Daily Dispatch and the highly respected Chronicle. There are soundbites from the President praising the PM for his improvisatory skills and maintaining magnanimously that once in a blue moon the occasional mouse has even been seen in the White House.

Nevertheless, The Chronicle's editorial thunders that the 'special relationship' has been irretrievably damaged.

It is the photographs of the mice milling about the carpet that are so breathtakingly marvellous. Really, these modern cameras! The definition is superb. Tom can even identify individual colleague. You could almost count their whiskers. Goods heavens, even George Milton, the former appeaser is there in the midst of it, rearing on his hind legs like a miniature warhorse.

Tom's favourite headline is :The Orb's:

MICE GALORE – PUSSY NO MORE!

After this there will be no more cats at Number Ten. There will be traps and poison again, of course, but Tom's mentor in Lincolnshire told him long ago how to deal with things like that. No, from now on, if they are relatively discreet, the mice will be able to go about their legitimate business again just like before.

And Tom can probably expect an earldom or a dukedom or some such bauble.

XII

It is two months later and Tom and the Prime Mouse are having lunch in the garden. It is Autumn now and the ivy at the back of the house is bright red in the security lights. Autumn means berries and windfall fruits.

It looks as if Brant-Broughton's government cannot survive a vote of no confidence in the new session of Parliament. It is not just a question of a chill in relations with America. Tom has fed Martin Spellar some rather salacious fabrications and he has leaked them to the press, who have come to have the highest respect for their mole. He no longer calls himself 'Fractal' by the way. In fact, he no longer works at Number Ten. It does not surprise Tom that Martin has become the Press Secretary and primary spin doctor to the Leader of the Opposition, who has a well-known aversion to cats, and whose eldest daughter has a pet rat.

'Tom,' says the Prime Mouse who is at work on a plum, 'you know that bit about Brant-Broughton and the ladies of the night? Was that you?'

'The prostitutes? Yes, that was me.'

'I mean was that really necessary?'

'Oh no, Stuart. It wasn't necessary at all. But it *was* rather fun don't you think?'

'Yes, yes, I suppose it was rather.'

They carry on nibbling companionably. After a while, the PM says: 'You know, I was chewing away at the leather on the back of that old chair in the entrance hall today (I think I might make rather a fine nest inside it one day) and it suddenly occurred to me that the cat smell has gone. It lingered for hell of a long time, didn't it.'

'It did, Stuart, it did.'

There is another ruminative pause.

'That was a cracking campaign of yours, you know, young mouse.'

'You're too kind, Sir.'

'Was it all your own idea, Tom? I mean did you not think of contacting MI5?'

'Mouse Intelligence 5? Are you joking?' Tom spits. 'They've become thoroughly incompetent. Can't even keep a secret these days. MI5! Huh!'

'I say, steady on, old rodent, keep your fur on and all that. No offence.'

'None taken.'

'So it *was* all your own idea?'

Tom tips his head to one side rather quizzically and nibbles at a patch of fur on his own haunch.

'Not *quite*,' he says. 'I did get a few tips from an old friend of mine who lives up in Lincolnshire.'

'Anyone I know?'

'I don't think you do, Stuart. I don't think you do. Though he was quite famous in his heyday,' says Tom wistfully.

'His name is Maximilian Emmanuel Lichtenheld.'

Acknowledgements

To those who have helped me with the writing and editing of these stories, I should like to extend my cordial thanks.

First to my dear, clever friend, Lyam Todd, who encouraged me to resume writing in the first place, who has patiently and creatively discussed ideas with me, and furnished not a few, and who is a most punctilious proof-reader and generous reviewer, thank you.

Thanks to my brilliant illustrator, Catherine Servonat-Blanc, who has captured Maximilian Emmanuel so perfectly on the cover.

For continued encouragement and support, I am ever grateful to Bill Clarke.

Massive thanks to my friends in the Dog and Bone Book Club for their constructive criticism.

And to all who have bought my work, or who are about to, thank you.

130 | The Mouse Triptych Ian Thomson

131 | The Mouse Triptych   Ian Thomson

133 | The Mouse Triptych Ian Thomson

Printed in Great Britain
by Amazon.co.uk, Ltd.,
Marston Gate.